Jamie Zaccaria

LAVENDER SPECULATION

Short Stories

WILDLING PRESS

ISBN: 978-1-957833-08-8
LCCN: 2023935591

Designed by Michael Hardison
Production managed by Christina Kann
Proofread by Mary-Peyton Crook and Grace Ball

Printed in the United States of America

Published by

www.wildlingpress.com

To everyone who couldn't find
what they wanted to read,
so they wrote it instead.

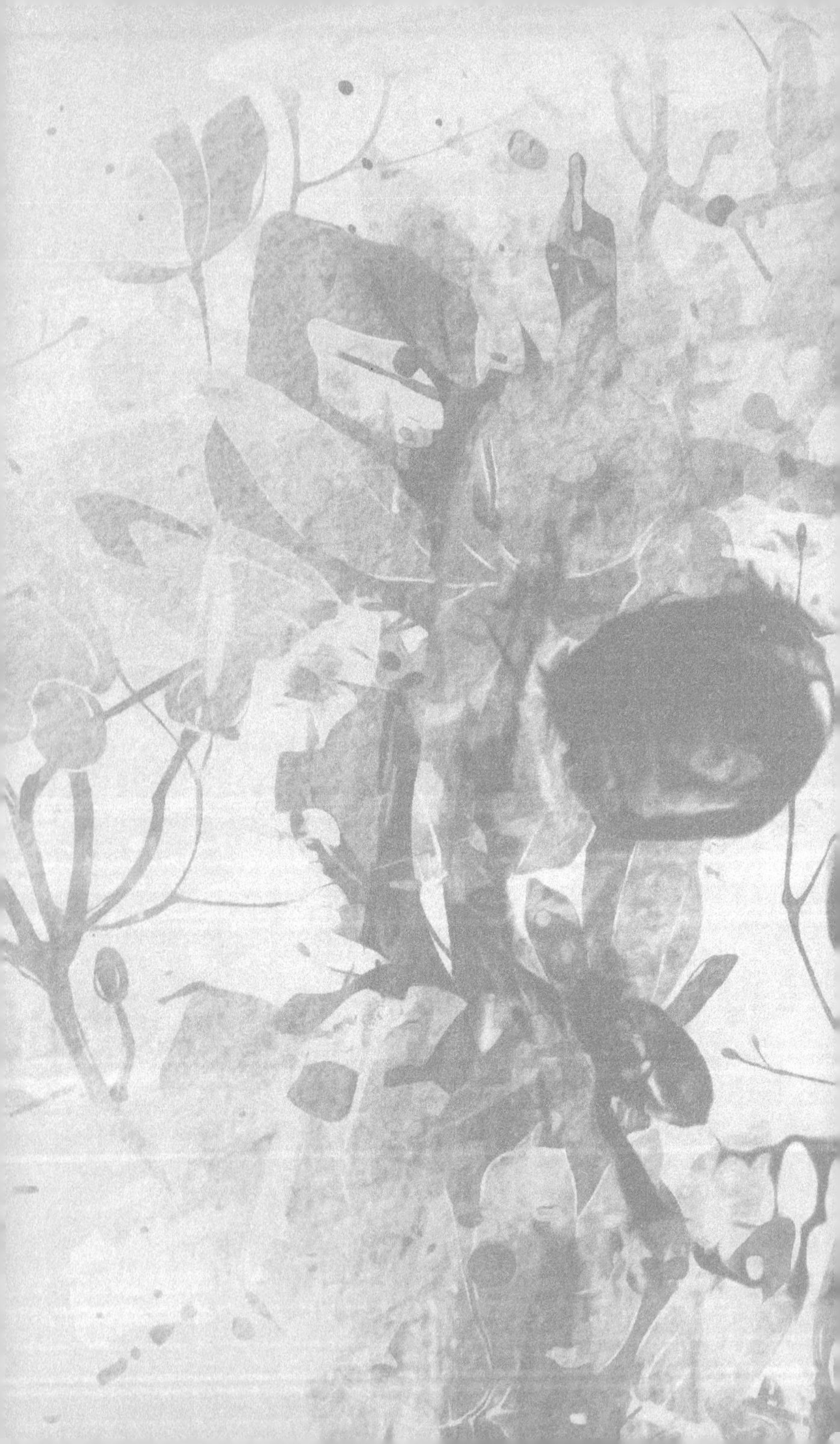

CONTENTS

The Witch of the Woods

I

She was a haggard old thing, smelling as dark and damp as the dwelling where she resided. Her matted gray hair hung about her shoulders, intermingled with layers of dried leaves and other debris from the forest. She had dirt under her fingernails, in her hair, and every place across her body; one could not tell where the soil ended and her skin began. Her eyes sunk deep into her face, the surrounding skin thin and lined with blue veins that barely shone through the filth. Covered in tattered black robes slung with belts from which various instruments dangled, she had all of her tools at her fingertips.

Here in her underground abode, she was the mistress of the past, the present, and the future. Here amongst the earthworms and gnarled tree roots, she could change the fate of something as small as a moth and as large as the death of a generation. The witch's thin, bony hands worked surprisingly rapidly, the long but mostly broken fingernails deftly removing leaves from stems on the smallest of herbs. Over the hearth, a black iron cauldron bubbled as it boiled with some concoction of ill intent. The fire crackled with intensity, providing warmth for her old bones and the power needed to bring her potions to life.

Unburdened as she was by the thought of bathing, beauty, or even sustenance, she moved surely through her residence. She tossed ingredients into the pot, throwing things aside that were of no use to her. She gingerly opened old glass jars filled with viscous liquids and body parts that had long ago withered into unidentifiable shapes.

The witch's home was buried deep in the woods. When she ventured outside, it was always after twilight, when the sun's full strength had faded away. The entire forest reacted to her presence, pulling away as if she were a disease. Roses withered and died at her touch. Birds fell silent when she walked by, their songs replaced with the sound of her boots crunching twigs underneath. Even the snakes would slither away from her, joining the deer and rabbits in their retreats.

She was the bringer of death, of ill omens and dark choices attached to darker desires.

She was always present in the village. Any time a sheep died mysteriously, or a child was born without breath, it was her name they whispered. She was disturbingly revered; in a way, the people almost prayed to her. Her mere existence could topple their entire lives. A word from her in their direction could poison their family.

She fed on the sacrifices of those spineless townspeople. They would leave her baskets of bread and apples at the edge of the woods. More importantly, they would leave her their unwanted babes, born in secret and out of wedlock or abandoned after being discovered disfigured.

Those who were brave enough to come to her were the most broken of souls. Only those who had been beaten down or had beaten down others to such a vulnerable position would dare look for the Witch of the Woods.

Today, it was a young girl—a woman, really—pale and slender, who appeared in the witch's doorway. Her brown-gold hair was tucked neatly into a stark-white bonnet. The cap's brightness contrasted against the dark fabric of her dress. These people were all alike; they pretended to be pious and good when just under the surface, they each burned with the desire to sin.

"Come in, child."

Prudence had chosen to visit the witch out of sheer desperation. She had made her mind up at Church. She had been helping to prepare baskets for the needy, working alongside her best friend. Each time her friend's head turned in Prudence's direction, it brought with it light brighter than the sun into her eyes. She'd had the overwhelming urge to kiss her, to press her small pink lips against Abigail's plump ones. Instead, she'd fled the Church into the rain, only stopping when she could no longer inhale cleanly.

Sitting in the mud as the rain poured down over her, Prudence had willed God to wash away the fire in her belly. She rued the joy that loving Abigail brought her. She hated that every time she laid eyes on the other woman, her stomach fluttered as if tiny gnats were flying around inside.

She loved Abigail, but she hated her even more. Prudence hated the control she had over her heart, her emotions, her very soul. She knew she had to rid herself of this evil attachment, not only because it was against the Word of God, but because she'd never be free until she did. That was when she had decided to visit the Witch of the Woods.

That morning—early, before the sun had risen into the sky—Prudence had made her way into the eastern woods for one last chance at salvation.

Now that she was there, she was almost regretting it. "Come in, child."

From the shadows, a withered hand gestured slowly, pointing sharp talons in Prudence's direction and willing her to move inside.

She felt the gravity of the earth itself holding her back, and yet she still moved forward, shaking with each step into that dirt-floor den. Every cell in her body screamed at her to turn back, but she pushed ahead anyway. She prayed silently, willing God to both send her deeper into the abyss and hold her back from it.

"There is no God here." The cracked voice broke the silence, delicate yet fierce.

Prudence gulped, eyes widening.

"What brings you to my home?" the witch asked,

staring directly into her eyes. The old woman's own were the palest blue and, despite being cloudy, pierced Prudence's very soul.

"I . . . I . . ." Prudence stuttered, unable to stop shaking. She took a deep breath and hardened her resolve. She had thought she'd known why she was here: to ask for her feelings to disappear. But deep down, she knew what she really wanted. "I need to make someone love me."

The witch cocked her head ever so slightly. "And what will you give me in return?" she asked.

Prudence knew she would not be able to trade something as simple as apples from her father's tree, or even a few coins, had she been able to come by them. She knew this deal would be made in sacrifice.

"Anything," she responded.

Without another word, the old woman turned to her table of assorted tools and ingredients. She bustled about, adding bits of herbs and drops of liquids to a small glass vial. Prudence did not know all of what went into the container, but she watched with horror as the witch wrung moisture from more than one dead animal.

The crone handed Prudence a scrap of paper no longer than her palm. Then she held out a raven's feather. Carefully, hesitantly, Prudence took the feather from the witch. The end was sharpened to a deadly point.

The witch gestured toward a seashell on the table that held a dark liquid. Prudence dipped the quill in it and then began her signature, realizing only after she had pressed point to paper that she was signing her name in blood.

The witch took the paper from Prudence and tucked it somewhere in the folds of her robes. She capped the vial and held it in the palm of her wrinkled hand.

"Mix this potion with some clay from the river. Form it into a figurine of the woman whose heart you wish to own and dry it in the sun. You must then tie a lock of her hair around it and place it under her bed. If it works, you will know immediately."

Prudence should have been shocked that the witch knew her forbidden love was for a woman, but she understood the secrets of sorcery ran deep.

"What if it doesn't work?"

The crone shrugged as if to say "oh well" and turned once more to pick up another item. It was a small piece of white lace—somehow pristine amidst the grime surrounding it.

"Offer this as a gift to your beloved," the witch instructed.

Prudence took in a breath. Lace was forbidden, but all the young women she knew secretly yearned for it to adorn their plain coifs.

She looked up to thank the witch, but the old lady had already moved deeper into her hollow, sending a silent message that their transaction had ended. Prudence turned and left.

II

Prudence made her way through the forest toward Reed Pond. They called it that because of the marsh plants that sprouted up around the water's edge. The farther she got from the witch's house, the more familiar and less threatening the woods felt. She wandered through the old-growth forest, noting empty hornets' nests hanging in trees and listening to the sound of a woodpecker drumming in the distance. Piles of small, oval pellets left by deer littered the forest floor.

The trees became sparser as she moved out of the forest and into a clearing where the pond bisected. She saw bluebirds feeding on crabapple trees on the edge of long patches of drying grass, gently swaying in the crisp autumn breeze.

The small watering hole was not too far from the edge of town but far enough to lend itself an air of privacy. Looking up, Prudence saw hawks swooping overhead, looking for prey down below. She imagined chipmunks and squirrels scurrying in the underbrush, hoping not to become targets while preparing their caches for winter.

She knelt by the edge of the murky water, wishing it were warm enough to spot a frog or turtle. It was too late in the season for these critters, and only the sturdiest animals remained about as the weather continued to chill. Prudence pushed her long gray sleeves up her arms and then began to dig into the thick, cold clay at the edge of the water. The slimy material squelched between her fingers as she worked.

Prudence grabbed a clump of the reddish substance, pouring in the vial's contents and kneading it as she would a fresh dough. She began shaping it into a young woman and her mind wandered back to her obsession.

She remembered when she and Abigail had lain together in a field of daisies mere months prior. The two had laughed, their fingers intertwined, and the breeze had whispered in their ears while bees flew by harmlessly. Prudence had turned her head to look at the woman beside her, and Abigail's face had shone brightly in the sun, her freckles dancing as her mouth moved. Prudence had wanted so badly to kiss her, but she hadn't dared to.

As her knees soaked up the cold and the wet from the ground, Prudence's memories of sunshine were chased away by memories of her minister's words.

"'All witchcraft comes from carnal lust, which in women is insatiable,'" he had quoted from a famous text she would never read. Prudence was beyond caring about her immortal soul. If witchcraft was the only way to have Abigail, then so be it.

III

"Idle hands are the Devil's playground," Prudence's mother reminded her for what felt like the tenth time that week. No sooner had she finished making a batch of soap then she was chided for not having yet picked up another task. There was never a shortage of work to do, tending the garden, weaving clothes, and pouring candles. She often helped her mother prepare meals for their large family, usually stews made from fish or game and whatever vegetables they had available.

They grew many different crops on their land: corn, cabbages, carrots, turnips, peas, pumpkin, and squash. She especially loved the apple trees, though, and she could sometimes even bake a pie, if there were enough apples. They also had a cow and a few pigs. They lived only half a mile from a small stream, to which Prudence would walk daily to collect fresh water. She often idled there, staring at her blurry reflection and scooping handfuls of cool, clear water into her mouth.

Her house was the same as the rest in town: made of wooden frames and facing southward to catch the sun. The family of eight all lived in the small abode together. Prudence's father was well respected in Church, and their family attended services at least twice a week.

The brick chimney opened up to a roaring fire, over which a large brass kettle swung. Her mother was preparing a stew for supper and letting it simmer in the heat. The rich scents of venison and vegetables wafted through the room, making Prudence's stomach rumble. However, hunger was not the most important thing on her mind.

Prudence yearned for some solitude outside of the

cramped home. She loved her family but often wished she could steal off to the woods to sit under an elm tree and read Cicero or Virgil quietly on her own. Even when there was time to indulge in these classics, she was frequently distracted by younger siblings crowding around her next to the hearth. As the oldest, she often watched after one or more of her five brothers and sisters.

Her father entered the room, then hung his musket up above the fireplace and warmed his hands for a few moments before turning toward his wife and children.

"I'm afraid I must be away to the meetinghouse. I will be back in time for prayers and supper," he told Prudence's mother. He put on his felt hat and kissed her mother squarely on the lips before leaving. Kissing one's wife in public was unseemly, but here in the privacy of their home, he showed affection to his spouse.

Prudence's cheeks blazed red when she caught herself imagining kissing Abigail. She knew that as a woman, she was more susceptible to temptation. The sins of Eve would easily manifest themselves in her descendants unless they maintained rigorous faith. Only by following the Church and praying daily could women find the courage and discipline they needed to stay on God's path. Unfortunately, she felt she had already strayed too far to ever find the path again.

Prudence also knew that she was expected to marry an upstanding man and bear him children. The thought terrified her. She remembered sitting beside her mother as she'd given birth to Hannah only a few years prior. No men had been allowed in the room, but some women had come from the village, bringing beer for the men and prayers to assist. Prudence had felt her mother's grip on her hand tighten as she'd pushed the babe forth. Her mother was pregnant again, and Hannah's birth had been difficult, so Prudence was worried about this one.

Her mother was in her sixteenth week of pregnancy, and she looked pale. The women of the village had said her pallor meant the child would be another girl. Prudence hoped not. She would not have wished the limitations of the weaker sex on any more of her siblings. She felt stifled by her life. Although it was the only one she had ever known, Prudence still yearned for something different.

She had been able to push those feelings away for so long, but the day she felt the first flame of desire for Abigail burn in her belly, she knew she could no longer fight her disappointment. If she had been born a man, she would have been better off. She could have attended town meetings and had a say in how her life would turn out.

Sighing, Prudence stretched her back and made her way outside to check on the garden. She looked up at the sky, an odd color of pale pink dispersed with angry-looking gray clouds. A snowstorm was coming. She would likely be stuck in the house for hours while they rode it out.

Suddenly, Prudence had an idea.

"Mother?" she asked, walking back inside. "I nearly forgot that I am due at the Smiths' this afternoon to help finish the charity alms of the season. With Mrs. Smith sick in bed, they need assistance preparing the final food and mending the baskets." She tried not to sound nervous.

"Of course, daughter. As God has given so freely of his Grace to us, must we help those who are needy. Pray you, bring Mrs. Smith these herbs, and tell her to make a tea of them. They should help with her cough." Her mother handed her a bundle of dried leaves.

"Yes, Mother." Prudence wrapped her thick wool cloak around herself and felt in its pocket to make sure the lace swatch and clay figurine were still there. She kissed her little sister on the forehead and left the house. The air was getting colder, and snow weighed heavily around her. A flock of geese flew by high above, their dark shapes forming the typical V-shape in the overcast gray sky.

IV

The Smiths' home was very similar to her own; pine shingles covered the roof, and windows closed by hinged casements. The last bits of sunlight that managed to shine through the impending storm bounced off their diamond-shaped panes of glass.

Prudence knocked, and one of Abigail's brothers let her inside. The fire was roaring, and the room was warm. She stepped carefully around the loom in the corner near the door as she entered, removing her coat and boots so as not to track water in behind her.

"Prudence!" Abigail called when she noticed her entrance, her smile lighting up her face. She hugged Prudence, then handed her a mug of warm cider, her hands gently brushing against Prudence's own, causing what felt like a jolt of electricity between them. Prudence felt her cheeks reddening, but Abigail seemed not to notice.

The two women settled down at the end of the table and immediately began working on the baskets. These were old ones that needed repairs before they could fill them with jars of pickled vegetables or loaves of bread.

"I have the most exciting news!" Abigail exclaimed, her face flushed with excitement. "I am going to marry Josiah Archer!"

Prudence felt her stomach drop out. She knew the despair could be read on her face, but she was too shocked to fight back.

Abigail was too distracted mending the basket to look up as she continued speaking. "My father is ever so happy. I have always known I would marry Josiah, ever since I was eight years old, and he named me the most beautiful girl in the village."

Prudence didn't want to listen anymore, yet she couldn't help but hang on every word. She stayed deathly still while Abigail prattled on, frozen in place with tears burning in her eyes.

Eventually, she stood up from her stool at the long

oak table. "But you're not yet twenty! Why rush into marriage when your mother needs you here?" Prudence's heart was racing, and she hoped her voice didn't betray the panic she felt.

"Many women are married at my age, and besides, Sarah is here to care for Mother," Abigail responded breathlessly. "It's all been decided. Minister Barrows will publish the banns to the public in next week's service."

Prudence imagined herself standing up in the middle of the crowded church, declaring her love as a reason to stop the wedding. She knew it was an impossible idea. Prudence could never let anyone know of her adoration for Abigail, lest she be restrained in stocks, whipped in the town square, or—worst of all—hanged as a sinner.

She spent the next hour holding back tears and making her shaking hands look busy while Abigail talked incessantly about her wedding and her future life. Each time she said the word "husband," it felt like a needle was piercing Prudence's heart. She tried to stay calm and remember the items in her pocket, praying they would work and turn her best friend's heart toward her and away from Josiah Archer.

By then, the storm had begun raging around them, the snow whirling in all directions. Traveling was soon out of the question. Mr. Smith insisted Prudence stay the night with them rather than attempt to make it back to her own house. This was not an uncommon occurrence during bad weather, and Prudence figured her mother would assume her daughter was safe and dry.

She joined Abigail and her family for supper and prayers before the two young women went off to bed. Usually, Abigail shared her bed with her younger sister, but the sister had been sent to stay with cousins a few towns over while their mother recovered from her illness. That meant she and Prudence had an entire four walls to themselves. The fact made Prudence's heart flutter.

Entering the cold room in the back of the house, Prudence ran her hand over the stack of books similar to those in her own home: the Bible and the psalm book and an almanac and the same New England Primer she'd used to learn to read. Sitting on top of the pile was a pair of sewing shears, just where they'd been the last time she'd visited. She softly grasped them.

Abigail was facing the window, concentrating on lighting the candles on the sill and babbling about having a house of her own. Prudence crept behind the girl and put out her hand, lightly fingering a curling lock of auburn hair. With shaking fingers, Prudence moved slowly to bring the scissors up to her friend's head, snipping the smallest piece and letting it fall into her other palm.

Abigail turned quickly, forcing Prudence to drop her hand, holding the scissors behind her back, nicking herself with the sharp instrument in the process. She tried not to cringe outwardly.

When Abigail turned away once more, Prudence set the shears on the end table. Then she quickly reached into her apron to tie the lock of hair around the crude clay figure.

Before Abigail could turn back around, Prudence tossed the figurine under her bed. She then removed the lace from her apron, holding it tightly in her palm as she continued to undress. Together, the two girls prepared for bed, removing their waistcoats and skirts. Next came the stiff petticoats, corsets, and wool stockings.

Feeling the cold air, Prudence rushed toward the bed, her bare feet touching the green rug's softness underneath. The two girls jumped under the covers, huddling together for warmth as they had done many times before.

They lay together under the patchwork quilt, feeling the warmth of the heated brick at their feet make its way up the bed. It was nothing compared to the fire Prudence felt inside her own body, a lethal mix of lust and envy. She held her breath, waiting for the figurine's magic to work its way up through the mattress and into Abigail.

"I have something for you," Prudence whispered to her best friend.

Abigail turned her head, and Prudence held out the scrap of lace. Abigail's eyes grew wide as she gently fingered it.

"Pru! How on earth did you come by this? It's beautiful!"

Prudence's heart fluttered, and she wondered if the spell was working yet.

"But surely, you must want to keep this for yourself," Abigail said, her green eyes rising to meet Prudence's brown ones.

The two sat up at the same time.

"No. I want you to have it," Prudence responded, folding the other woman's fingers over the delicate trim.

Abigail leaned forward and kissed Prudence on the forehead. "Thank you, Pru. You are my best friend in the whole world."

Without any thought, Prudence leaned forward and kissed Abigail squarely on the mouth. Abigail's lips opened in shock, and for a brief moment, she seemed to kiss back. Then, suddenly, she pushed Prudence away.

"What are you doing?" Abigail demanded. Her face was flushed, eyes narrowed. She wiped the back of her hand across her lips, dropping the lace onto the bed.

"I . . . I thought . . ." Prudence stammered.

Abigail stared at her with a look of complete incomprehension. The very air around her seemed tense.

"I love you," Prudence said quietly.

Abigail looked horrified. Immediately, Prudence knew that no matter what magic she cast or gifts she gave, nothing would make her best friend love her in the same way.

"You're a filthy sinner!" Abigail hissed, not shouting loud enough to wake her father, but the venom in her voice was potent.

Prudence's eyes filled with tears. She jumped out of bed and raced out of the door, out of the house, and into the forest.

V

She ran faster than she knew she could, into the woods whose darkness seemed blacker than the depths of the sea. She felt branches scratch her skin and smack her face, but they didn't slow her down. She ran until she'd left the entire town behind. As she was dressed only in her nightgown, the cold bit at her skin, yet Prudence never slowed her pace. There was snow on the ground and in the air, and its stark white color contrasted sharply with the black, twisted tree branches.

Prudence continued running until her lungs ached and her legs were bloodied and bruised from all the stones and logs she'd crashed against. She raced until she saw spots in her eyes, and then she ran some more. Not even the call of a nearby wolf pack could stop Prudence as she barreled toward her destination. She willed the rapacious canines to come near her, and if they had, she would have held her arms out in submission and sacrificed herself to the creatures who had surely been sent by the Devil to test her faith. Prudence knew she had no covenant with God, not anymore.

Her mind reached back into her childhood as she ran—climbing trees with her brothers, hugging her calico doll close on stormy nights, and secretly running her fingers along her grandmother's tortoiseshell combs from England. That innocent child no longer existed. Now, she was merely the shell of a woman, carved out and filled with ugly envy and desire. Before now, Prudence would never have imagined herself turning to the one person she feared the most in this world, the Witch of the Woods. Witches performed filthy carnal acts with demons, but how could she—who had dreamt of sinful, sensual acts with Abigail—be any different? If sorcery was an assault from Satan, then Prudence would join the Devil's pact.

Panting, both frozen from the cold and burning with emotion, Prudence pushed her way into the half-sunken abode of the witch. She was not surprised to find the woman sitting in a chair, staring as if she already knew who was coming. The smile she offered up was devoid of any warmth.

Prudence opened her mouth to speak but found she could not force any words out of her throat. The witch gave her a look that said she already understood why she was there. She stood up from the chair, the fire jumping higher as she rose. The Witch of the Woods picked up a silver blade that glittered in the light from the flames. She handed it to Prudence.

Without exchanging any words, Prudence knew what she needed to do. The instructions flowed smoothly into her mind as the knife exchanged owners.

Her hands, which not moments before had been trembling with fear, cold, and exhaustion, now held the blade firmly. Without hesitation, Prudence lifted it to her chest. She tore open the front of her nightgown, exposing her sternum to the air that swirled with the heat from the raging fire. She pressed the tip of the rusted knife to her skin, pushing down through white layers until a red rivulet began to form.

Prudence pressed harder, feeling bones break and tissue split through as the weapon pierced her flesh and made its way to her most vital of internal organs. Bright scarlet blood ran down her hands, over her delicate wrists and pale forearms, cascading over her body and onto the ground. Dropping the knife to the floor, she reached inside the hollow of her chest and through the sharp ribs. She found the beating organ and grasped it, pulling it free.

The heavy emotions of longing and unrequited love floated away from her like ashes on the wind. She felt their burden lifted and knew that, finally, the spell had worked.

Prudence held out her heart, dense and dark, and covered in a thin, translucent sac. Below her, the flames spat and crackled, the light reflecting in her brown eyes. She continued to feel nothing. Her once-white nightgown was stained vermillion, but she felt none of the lightness that should have come with her life force draining from her body. The black cavern in her chest rose and fell steadily as she miraculously continued to breathe. Prudence felt no pain, no pressure, no lack of any vital life-giving organ.

She tossed her heart into the fire. She was free.

My New Gown

My new gown is spectacular, fit for a queen. It's soft and warm with pink fur that feels like the lightest of touches, held with love. The bodice is satin, so smooth and sensuous I can't stop running my fingers over its seductive surface.

I take it off the mannequin, and immediately its warmth spreads through my fingers, up my arms, and into my heart. Its heat beats through my veins to every limb, like the comfort of a fireplace on a winter's day or of a mother's hug after many months apart. It is the feeling of safety and belonging, and love.

My new gown is nothing like my old one. That one was tight and shiny, and looked as if it were on fire. It may as well have been aflame for how it burned through my skin, leaving charred holes looking down into my organs, laid bare and vulnerable. It was the gown of a courtesan fooled into believing her self-worth was nothing more than what she could provide for others.

For too long, I was terrified to remove that blood-red gown for fear it would peel away my outsides with it, leaving me nothing but a ruined skeleton. I kept it on as it rotted away, taking pieces of my flesh with it. I lost color as the old gown bled me dry from the outside in. Like a burning constrictor, it stole my breath and my will to live.

Eventually, I grew bolder, enough that I decided to determine my own fate. I determined I would not like this ensemble of flames and despair to eat away at every last cell of my body. I knew it was deadly as much as I was afraid to untangle it from my own cutaneous layers.

One day, I found the courage to remove the old gown. And once I did, I found myself capable of healing. My skin came back glowing and healthy, my organs protected by layers of fat and tissue. Strength exuded from the ligaments through the fasciae, connecting my pieces into the one whole person that I had been missing for so long.

And on top of my beautiful new figure is my new gown, comfortable and kind and flattering. Shades of coral and blush and rose and petal pink envelope my being. It feels as if it should always have been part of me. It feels as if I should never take it off, and I don't think I ever will. It feels like home.

A Necessary Procedure

Rachel approached the front desk, signed in, and took a seat on the couch. The waiting room was crisp and clean. Her heart beat rapidly, and she wondered if it would continue to do so after the procedure was complete.

Squirming, Rachel took a deep breath. She knew this was a big decision, but otherwise she felt helpless. She was at the end of her rope with this relationship. Something had to change, and Sarah had made it clear that it would not be her. It had fallen, then, to Rachel to take drastic measures to preserve what could be described as true love.

Rachel told herself it wouldn't be so bad. These were the best doctors in NYC, and this procedure was their specialty. This clinic had even been on the cover of *Time* magazine. She certainly was not the first person to have this done, and she knew she wouldn't be the last.

On the coffee table was a copy of the clinic's catalog. It advertised their services alongside a smiling couple with perfectly straight, white teeth.

"Be the best person you can be."

"Create the perfect relationship."

"Live happily ever after."

That last one made her cringe. As a child, Rachel had been a fan of fairy tales. She'd liked that the beautiful princess and the handsome prince always managed to "live happily ever after." Even after Rachel grew up and realized she preferred princesses to princes, she still liked those romantic endings. It made sense when things ended with two merged as one, like a book closing in finality rather than frustration.

Rachel thumbed through the catalog, reading over the stuff she already knew about the procedure. It would be a very intense process overall. She had spent months planning, saving money, and passing psych evaluations. She had worked with her doctor to specify the exact measurements and calculations they would use. Now the day was finally here.

She turned to an article on the benefits of the procedure for relationships. One couple had raved that the process had pulled them back from the brink of divorce. Another had claimed they hadn't had a single argument since. One man had even said it'd turned his wife into the person he'd always wanted to marry.

The doctors claimed that the procedure would ultimately ensure couples live happily together for many years.

Rachel's pulse quickened and heat flooded her face, but she took deep breaths. A pair of shoes squeaked from the hallway as they approached the reception desk.

"Rachel Wong?" called a nurse with a clipboard.

He wore perfectly pressed white scrubs and a vacant expression.

Rachel got up and silently followed the man down a long hallway and into an examination room. She sat down and was handed a piece of paper full of numbers.

"Please read through all of your predetermined calculations and sign off that it is all correct. The doctor will be in shortly." The nurse left and closed the door behind him. Rachel sighed as she stared down at her paperwork, rereading the choices she had made a week ago. She wanted to be careful not to go too far in changing certain personality traits. She had requested they reduce her jealousy and possessiveness, tone down her anger, and increase her happiness.

Looking around, Rachel spotted an array of needles next to a box of latex gloves. She saw a fancy-looking monitor next to a drill connected to more wires than her entertainment system at home. Instruments ranging in size from sewing needles to turkey basters lined the countertops, each untouched and perfectly sealed in a plastic pouch.

Not wanting to look at the instruments anymore, Rachel picked up her phone and scrolled through the photos of her and Sarah. The two women had done nothing but argue for the previous two months. Rachel's mind wandered six weeks back, to the night of their biggest fight. She remembered most of the evening in painful detail, the hurt and anger rising up in her chest alongside the memory.

"Babe, you home?" Rachel shouted as she walked in the door, kicking off her shoes and throwing the mail down on the coffee table. She made her way through the sunny apartment the two had shared for about eight months. When they'd first moved in together, there'd been a few weeks of the "honeymoon period." They'd been happy and in love and never argued about anything.

Rachel walked into the bathroom and found Sarah applying mascara. Music was playing on her phone, and she was wearing a sparkly halter top and tight jeans.

"Are we supposed to be going out tonight?" Rachel asked.

"No," Sarah replied without taking her eyes off the precise makeup application in the mirror. "But Beth just called and invited me to this show downtown. She had an extra ticket. I thought you had to work late."

"I did, but I got out early. I wanted to surprise you," Rachel replied with a prickly tone. She could feel the static in the air that preceded an argument.

Sarah turned around to look at her girlfriend. "Oh, well, you don't mind if I go, right?" she asked, but it sounded less like a question and more like a statement.

"Um, I guess not." Rachel trailed off as she walked into the kitchen.

Of course, Sarah was going out without her. Last time she'd gone out with her friends without her, Sarah had come home wasted hours after she'd said she'd be back, laughing at inside jokes that Rachel didn't understand. It had been a long, stressful, exhausting day for Rachel, and she'd been looking forward to spending the night with her girlfriend.

Sarah came storming into the kitchen after her, and before she even spoke, Rachel knew what she would say.

"What's your problem?"

"I don't have a problem," Rachel snapped back. She was opening cabinets and slamming them closed haphazardly, not really looking for anything but itching to keep her hands busy to stop herself from crying.

"Why can't you trust me? You're always so jealous!" Sarah's voice fell into her usual defensive tone, the words on autopilot by now, her arms crossed.

"Maybe I don't trust you because you're not trustworthy," Rachel yelled back. She immediately regretted it; each time they came back to this topic, it stung more than the last.

"That was months ago. I'm sorry. I've been better," Sarah replied, a little quieter.

"It's not about trusting you; it's just . . . I thought we could spend the night together, and instead, you're going out without me. Again." Being left out hurt, but what was worse was the familiar sense of secrecy creeping up underneath.

Sarah didn't respond for a few seconds. She blinked, her face frustratingly unreadable to Rachel.

"If you can't move past this and trust me, we're never

going to work out," she said. Her dark eyes were shining with tears, but she stood tall, and her chin jutted out.

Rachel didn't have a retort to that. Sarah was right, of course. Rachel had to let her anger and jealousy go if the relationship was going to work, but no matter how hard she tried, she couldn't. She couldn't stop those emotions from creeping into her mind and out of her mouth and ruining everything.

"Hello, Ms. Wong. How are you?" the doctor asked as she entered the room, pulling Rachel from her memory. Rachel wiped her eyes and put her phone facedown on her lap, smiling up at the doctor. She hadn't told Sarah about what she was doing, and she felt guilty for lying.

She could barely hear the doctor's follow-up questions over the thunderous rush of blood in her ears. She was starting to get hot and could feel beads of sweat forming on her forehead. Rachel was sitting up, wearing a hospital gown and a hair bonnet with a one-inch opening where the needle would go. It was at her nape, on the underside of her hairline, so she hoped her partner wouldn't notice the bit of hair they'd have to shave off.

The doctor, a tall woman in her mid-forties, explained the details of the procedure again as she put on gloves and readied a syringe. She had gone through most of this information at the previous appointment, but not quite in this amount of detail.

Rachel knew the laser technology wasn't yet perfect. They still needed to drill a hole in her skull to maneuver the lasers around her gray matter. She closed her eyes and pretended like that wasn't the most daunting thing she'd ever had to imagine happening to her body.

The procedure itself was terrifying despite being painless. Rachel was awake throughout, watching as green and red lasers pinpointed various spots on her forehead. She heard the menacing sound of a drill but couldn't see it. Thank God for the anesthetic and lack of nerve endings in brain tissue. Rachel saw calculations on the screen changing, going up and going down.

All of a sudden, her senses heightened in fear, and she was keenly aware of the cold in the air, the blank eyes of the surgeons staring down at her, the menacing sound of the drill coming ever closer. Her heart began racing and Rachel felt heat rush through her body. She took a deep breath, trying to stay calm, and closed her eyes.

Sarah's face was behind her eyelids, from the day they first met. Rachel could smell that familiar citrus scent and heard her husky laugh. They were back at that bar, Sarah smiling coyly and tilting her head at her as she asked for her number. Her eyes sparkled, and Rachel felt the familiar butterflies in her stomach.

Comatose Beauty

At first there was only darkness. Darkness and the incessant *beep-beep-beep*ing. Gradually I could see again, but not from my own eyes. I viewed my own body from above, as it laid on the hospital bed, eyes closed and breathing steady. I had no concept of how long I had been here, in the ether of nothingness that my mind seemed to exist in, while my broken body laid beneath me.

"Sorry, I fell asleep," came a voice.

My vision focused, and I saw a boy sitting in the uncomfortable-looking chair near the end of the—my—bed. I was sure that I had never met him before, but somehow I knew he'd spent much of his time here. He was a handsome stranger whose presence was intrinsically linked to the white room I existed in. Sometimes he just sat there, but often, he would talk to me, telling me stories or simply recounting the events of his day. The sound of his voice was like a soothing prayer to my consciousness that floated so far from my actual body.

Today he was talking a lot. From the odd angle I saw of his face, I thought he was cute. He looked like he was in his late teens, with dark hair and eyes and a charmingly crooked smile. My heart ached that I could not smile back, that I could not respond to his questions or his stories. It was as if an invisible barrier stretched between us, preventing my phantom any participation in this human experience.

From his visits, I was able to learn about his life. He told me about his childhood in the suburbs with the golden retriever named Chance, who he seemed to love very much. He entertained me with funny stories, and if I'd had a voice, I would have laughed in response. When he spoke to me, I no longer felt the rush of adrenaline from the car crashing or heard the rain plopping on the windows followed by tires screeching. When I listened to him, I was in his world and not laying in a hospital bed.

I had no memories of things that happened before the accident or questions of what the future might hold for me. I was uncertain of when—or if—I would ever wake up. Whenever I began to grow somber with these things, his voice sliced through my inner thoughts, battling the uncertainty and keeping my *beep-beep-beeping* going steady.

One day he came into my room and sat in his familiar green chair, but he did not talk to me right away. His face was sullen, forehead wrinkled, and his eyes held so much pain I thought I could feel it through the air. His shoulders slumped, and he was still for a long time.

Eventually he spoke: "My grandfather died today."

So that was why he was always at the hospital. I wondered why he'd spent so much time in my room instead of his grandfather's.

As if he could read my unconscious mind, the young man said next, "I knew it would happen. I've visited him every day for a year, since they said he was going to die. He sleeps mostly . . . or slept, I guess. That's how I first found you; he was sleeping, so I went wandering the halls. I knew he was going to die eventually, but it still hurts. I still miss him."

My heart went out to this beautiful, sad boy in my room. I felt for his loss but also for my own because of what I knew he would say next.

"I guess that means I won't be coming to visit you anymore." He placed his hand gently on my arm, running his thumb along my wrist.

At his words I felt a strange rush of energy. This mystery boy was more than just my knight; he was my anchor to the real world. My steady *beep-beep-beeping.* My friend.

"When I first found your room, the nurses told me you might wake up one day, and I could try talking to you." He stood up and moved toward my bed. Gently, the boy bent down and kissed my pale forehead. I felt like crying and wished that ghosts could shed tears.

He whispered in my ear, "I'm sorry I couldn't help you. But thank you for listening."

There was a strange and sudden vacuum effect. It felt as if all my insides were strewn about in the air and suddenly thrown back into my body. I couldn't see anymore, but I felt a pulling sensation akin to gravity, then a sudden stop, like my spirit had collided with something.

My eyes fluttered open, and I was me again. My limbs felt heavy and unnatural, and my mouth tasted sour. The beep-beep-beeping still rang in my ears. I was in my body, and he was standing in front of me with a look of astonishment on his face. My knight in shining armor smiled at me. I smiled back.

A Killer Brunch Special

Sadie Mousavi was not looking forward to the "bimbo brunch," as she called the event she'd been dreading for the past week. Her girlfriend, Bess, had begged her to come along with her and five of her work friends. Sadie had met these women before and frankly detested their company. However, they'd invited her along to brunch multiple times now, and she'd run out of excuses for not going. Plus, she knew it would make Bess happy, so she had begrudgingly caved.

She felt comfy in her favorite pair of boyfriend jeans and sapphire blue blouse. Luckily, the weather was warm enough that she no longer needed to wear a heavy jacket. After exiting the L train, Sadie made her way up to the street, breathing in the not-so-fresh Brooklyn air that was at least cleaner than anything she'd inhaled down in the subway. She walked a few blocks until she met Bess in front of a small establishment called the Secret Garden.

Dressed in a bright yellow floral-print sundress topped with a denim jacket, Bess was easy to spot from down the street. Sadie's ladylove was obsessively running her hands through her new haircut. She'd recently chopped her dark blonde locks into a pixie that was undeniably adorable but would still take some time for Sadie to get used to.

They entered the restaurant. Waiters were rushing around, still arranging place settings and getting the dining area in order. Mackenzie, the self-appointed leader of the gang, had insisted they get there right when the place opened to ensure them a place among the very limited outside seating, so they were the first group to be brought to their table.

The hostess led them through the main seating area and into a small, enclosed outdoor courtyard. They were clearly going for "quaint village," but it came off more like a museum exhibit of what contemporary Americans imagined 1950s Paris to look like. There were only a handful of tables, and two had been pushed together for their large group.

Sadie recognized the tall woman who was just sitting down at the table as they walked in. Her name was Fatima. She was speaking rapidly to a woman with blonde curls across the table. Without pausing her monologue, Fatima sat down, awkwardly pulling her plaid miniskirt back down her thighs as it rode up.

"Hello, ladies!" Mackenzie half-spoke, half-sung to the two women when they approached.

Bess tried to organically reintroduce Sadie to the rest of the group.

The blonde was Lauren. Her annoying valley girl accent complemented her Barbie-esque ensemble of a cropped, gray knit top and pink tulle skirt. She was sitting next to a beautiful dark-skinned woman who Sadie remembered as being the only one from the group she had enjoyed talking to—besides Bess, of course. Her name was Alicia, and she greeted the two with a warm smile and a wave from her green-pleather-jacket-clad arm.

Paz was the quietest of the women, if only because her attention could rarely be pulled away from the metallic gold iPhone practically glued to her hands. Her impeccably groomed eyebrows moved up and down with expressions to match the endless conversation she seemed to be having over text. When she did address the rest of them, she tugged at one of the many thin gold necklaces adorning her bronzed collarbones.

Then there was Mackenzie: the uber-bitch herself. With her annoyingly perfect platinum ponytail and icy blue eyes, she looked like a Wakefield twin. Naturally, the queen bee of the friend group was wearing a pair of yoga pants that probably cost more than Sadie would spend on groceries for two weeks. More than anything, she was the reason why Sadie didn't want to spend any of her precious weekend time here.

The last time Sadie had encountered Mackenzie and the rest of these colleagues had been at Bess's housewarming party a few months ago. Mackenzie had gone from corner to corner of the apartment, making passive-aggressive comments about how "cute" it was that Bess used second-hand furniture for decorating. Maybe her girlfriend was oblivious to the utterly rude way her coworker was acting, but Sadie was not. It had taken all her willpower not to punch the woman in the face right there.

Sadie glued on her smile and quickly locked her eyes on the pitcher of mimosa on the table. After their standard hugs hello to everyone, Bess and Sadie sat together and filled their glasses with the citrus champagne cocktail. Sadie thought about getting a coffee but decided alcohol would work just as well.

A bored-looking waiter approached the table and began his speech before asking if they were ready to hear it. "Our brunch special today is the steak tartare and shaved egg crostini. It's adapted from Sigmund Freud's famously favorite breakfast meal."

Sadie rolled her eyes. Only in Williamsburg would they use a misogynistic pseudo-scientist to sell overpriced, undercooked brunch items.

"That sounds literally amazing," Mackenzie squealed. "I need it."

Fatima and Paz echoed her order, and Lauren took a minute to consider it, then threw her hands up in mock exasperation and said, "Why not, I guess?"

Alicia followed up by ordering a Greek omelet with extra olives, and Bess decided on the blueberry crepes. Sadie was last.

"I'll have the tomato and avocado toast, no brie, please," she said, handing the waiter her menu before he walked away.

"I'm absolutely starving; I ran five miles this morning," Mackenzie told the group, who responded with varying levels of faux interest. It turned out that most of them belonged to a running group, although Mackenzie, always the overachiever, had done this morning's run on her own.

She turned to address Sadie. "You absolutely must join our running group! We get together three times a week, and right now, I'm even training for a marathon!"

Sadie forced a smile. "Thanks for the invite, but I don't run."

"But you really should! Exercise is so good for you!" Mackenzie was barely hiding her patronizing tone.

"I exercise plenty; I just hate running," Sadie said firmly.

Thankfully, the waiter interrupted Mackenzie before she could continue in her fruitless efforts. He bent to refill their champagne glasses from the mimosa pitcher, allowing Fatima a chance to begin talking about her favorite topic: her boyfriend, Ryan.

Eventually, the food arrived. There was a moment of silence as the women began eating, followed by the usual discussion of whose dish was satisfying. Mackenzie, Lauren, Paz, and Fatima were all in agreement that the special was indeed amazing. Fatima offered a bite to Alicia, who ate it and nodded in support before turning back to her eggs. Lauren tried to get Bess to taste the steak tartare, but she politely declined, mouth already full of blueberry.

"Sadie, how about you?" Lauren asked before immediately remembering her dietary preferences. "Oh, never mind; sorry, I forgot you're a vegan."

"No worries," Sadie responded. The bubbly was

kicking in, and, with a delicious meal in front of her, she was actually starting to relax a little bit. These certainly weren't the type of people she enjoyed spending time with, but it was nice to be out with Bess, and avocado was her favorite food, after all.

The conversation once again revolved around significant others, with Mackenzie subtly reminding everyone that her fiancé was exceedingly rich and Lauren sighing over being single yet again. Fatima took advantage of the change of topic to again gush over her single favorite human being. She started explaining their upcoming trip to the Hamptons.

Mid-sentence, Fatima paused. A funny look came across her face before she suddenly projectile-vomited a chunky blood-colored substance, turning her white turtleneck a bright scarlet.

The rest of the women jumped up quickly out of their seats. Half of the table was covered in a sticky substance that smelled of bile and copper. Time seemed to stop as the women all tried to comprehend the situation.

"Oh my god, Fatima, are you okay?" Lauren moved to help her friend.

The others exchanged worried glances, unsure of what to do.

Fatima coughed and let out a strange gurgle that sounded like a growl. Then she lunged at Lauren, her bloodied mouth making rough contact with the other woman's neck.

Lauren attempted a scream, and suddenly everyone was in motion. Sadie and Alicia rushed forward to pull Lauren away, while Bess cautiously tried to remove Fatima from their friend. Bess quickly gave up when she realized her coworker was not only stronger than any twenty-something-woman had any right to be, but was using both her manicure and pearly whites as deadly weapons.

A crash sounded from inside the restaurant and Fatima startled, dropping Lauren and staring at the door like a cat who senses a mouse nearby. Lauren was clutching her neck while blood spurted through her fingers, sobbing as Alicia tried to comfort her. The other girls stared at Fatima with shocked expressions.

Suddenly, Fatima whipped her head back toward the group and lunged at them. While the others backed off, Sadie pushed a chair in front of the woman, causing the dark-haired beast to fall over it. The obstacle gave them enough time to huddle together in the corner, but it only seemed to enrage Fatima more.

Just as Sadie was contemplating how she could use brute force to prevent her own neck from being bitten open, she heard a groan of pain from her left side. Turning, she saw Paz doubled over. Pink foam had begun to ooze from her mouth. Paz stood again, her eyes dilated, back hunched, and teeth bared. Bess and Mackenzie backed away from their friend and closer to Sadie.

Paz turned toward them, her perfect manicure now brandished like deadly claws.

"What the fuck is going on?" screamed Bess as the

two animal-women came toward the group.

Without thinking, Sadie grabbed a steak knife from the table, brandishing it while the other girls moved behind her.

"Stay back!" she screamed shakily. Sadie had never stabbed anyone before, but in light of the situation, she figured there was a first time for everything. Neither Fatima nor Paz seemed to hold any recognition of the others in their eyes. Both stared at the rest of their group with nothing but bald hunger. These were no longer women but bloodthirsty creatures who would tear them to pieces. Sadie's resolve hardened, and she took charge.

"Grab a weapon!" she screamed as Paz lunged at her. Sadie swiped with the knife, slicing off a chunk of Paz's cheek, its contour still shining as the piece of flesh fell to the ground.

From behind her, Sadie heard the sounds of a struggle but couldn't take her eyes off the snarling creature in front of her. Paz barely registered the injury, intent only on making contact with Sadie's flesh.

Sadie tightened her grip on the knife, pulled back her arm, and jammed as hard as she could, this time aiming for Paz's throat. Blood spurted from the wound, her neck gaping open and pulsing where the knife stuck out. Then suddenly, she fell to the floor.

Sadie swung around, expecting to see the other four girls facing off against Fatima, but instead she was greeted with a more horrifying scene. Bess was brandishing a chair in the air, barely keeping Fatima away from her. Instead of backing her up, Alicia and Mackenzie were on the other side of the courtyard, running in circles from Lauren, whose hands had moved away from her gushing neck wound and instead were attempting to claw the other women's skin. She had the same crazed, bloodshot eyes as the other two.

Swearing in Farsi under her breath, Sadie moved to help Bess. Together, they used the chair to herd Fatima into the corner. Sadie frantically looked around for a weapon, whipping her head around so fast that she was temporarily blinded by her brown curls. She grabbed the closest thing to her—a champagne flute—and smashed it on the side of the table. Then, with Bess pinning Fatima down with the legs of the faux antique chair, Sadie smashed the broken glass into the creature's eyeball with only a slight hesitation. Fatima let out an inhuman screech as the shard sunk through her eye socket, gooey liquid seeping out around it, before sinking to the ground.

Dropping the chair, Bess grabbed onto Sadie. Together, they made their way toward Alicia and Mackenzie, who were taking turns smashing Lauren with an array of objects. They reached the others just as Alicia slammed a serving dish into Lauren's head, forcing her down hard. Her skull cracked against the brick wall, and this time she didn't get up again.

"We have to get out of here," Sadie said, motioning for the two to follow her. She briefly had the presence of mind to wonder why no one had come into the court-yard to help them after hearing the screams. Immediately upon entering the main dining hall, she knew why.

The scene was a madhouse. The main dining room was full of people in motion—half of them covered in blood and screeching animalistic tones. The other half were running for their lives or else had already become menu items themselves. The four women seemed to realize at once that the front door was too far away for them to make it out.

Turning toward the others, Sadie began to speak, "Through the kitch—" but was interrupted as a frenzied middle-aged woman jumped on Alicia from behind. Alicia screamed, but in a matter of seconds, her attacker ripped out her throat and the sound turned into a gurgle.

Bess and Mackenzie cried out in shock, but Sadie's instincts took over. Grabbing the other two by the arms, she pulled them to the side and into the kitchen.

There were fewer bodies in there but also less visibility, as an island of cooking implements covered in hanging utensils blocked her view. Thankfully, the back door was wide open.

Suddenly, Mackenzie stopped moving. After a brief pause, she hunched over a sink and began vomiting. Sadie had the urge to upchuck herself but tried to focus and stay calm. The scents of cooking onions and maple syrup converged into a sickening addition to the smell of rotting flesh and flowing blood seeping in from the dining room.

Then Mackenzie was no longer Mackenzie; she had succumbed to whatever infestation was taking over half the restaurant. She was a monster like the rest of their party. She stood between them and the back door, her eyes bloodshot, the redness somehow creeping into the irises themselves.

"We have to make a run for it!" Bess shouted. "Try to get past her!"

The door on the other side of the kitchen was blocked by more than just steel towers covered in hot plates as Mackenzie snarled her way toward them. If Sadie could only avoid the blond woman, they could try to escape through the back door. But there was not much room in the kitchen, and no way could they both be fast enough to maneuver around her.

Sadie thought quickly, and her head turned left and right. Her eyes fell on an iron skillet in the sink, and she quickly moved to grab it. Brandishing it like Rapunzel, she stepped in front of Bess to shield her.

She swung hard, slamming the skillet into Mackenzie's head until her brains splattered the wall behind them.

"I told you," Sadie breathed, covered in blood and gray matter, "I don't run."

Hand in hand, Sadie and Bess walked out of the back door and into the fresh air.

Eviscerate

He meant to eviscerate her with his words. He wanted to use his pen to bleed her dry. As he pulled the instrument across the paper, he imagined a knife across the surface of her skin, the ink bleeding like blood, black running onto red.

He wanted to destroy her from the inside out, not just physically but through the core of her being. He wanted to use words to unwrap everything she was within, her brain and her heart and her soul, until she had nothing left but little flutters of paper in the wind that would soon dissolve into even less than nothing.

He was a writer, but—according to her—not a good one. For eight hours a day, he went to work only to be beaten down verbally, deflated emotionally, and sucked dry of his creativity. For eight hours a day, five days a week, he was told time and again how terrible he was at his passion. Now he wrote with a single-minded goal: to eviscerate her.

Maybe he was a bad man, but he didn't care because it felt good to be bad. It felt good to imagine his writing, the thing she hated the most, being the thing to destroy her. It felt so good to use what he knew was his power to prove that he was not the lowly scum she made him feel like every day. He needed to prove he could create worlds, but more than that—he could destroy with his writing.

Tonight, he took his revenge. Sitting in the near dark with only a small candle illuminating the pages, he wrote furiously. As the words piled on the page, they darkened the white sheet in front of him. He knew he was destroying her with his vocabulary, but what he didn't realize until this moment was that, as she lifted from the page of tangible life, so did he. As the words spilled out of him, the cells of his cutaneous layer up-ended themselves from his body. He was eviscerating her but also himself.

Lips as Red as Blood

I always knew there was something wrong with my stepmother. I knew she did something strange in the lowest level of our castle; I could hear the screams at night. They rose up from the basement, so loud that their residue lingered in my bedroom two floors up.

When my father married her, she was beautiful like an ice statue. She never ate, she never danced, and she never laughed. She was a pristine sculpture whose interest was only piqued by the reflection she spotted when walking by a mirror.

Then my father died, and everything changed. She turned from ice to fire, burning up everything and everyone in her path. She chased away his closest advisors and replaced them with somber-faced men from foreign countries who rarely spoke. A darkness soon spread over the entire kingdom—not just a feeling of despair but eventually a tangible pattern of death. Each year the harvest yielded fewer crops, the children grew more sickly, and even the sun seemed farther away.

She seemed to hate happiness, banning the dinners and balls my father used to love. What she hated most of all, though, was me. The older I got, the more enraged she became at merely laying eyes on me. I used to sleep in the west wing near the king's quarters, but I was quickly moved down a floor, demoted to a position physically and socially lower than bequeathed to me by my heredity. My handmaidens were removed, and I was no longer given an allowance to buy new clothing. Eventually I was no longer treated as royalty at all. I was only another young girl scuttling through the corridors avoiding the queen's wrath.

As I got older, people started to notice me again. They whispered about how beautiful I was and how much I looked like my mother. Hearing this only enraged my stepmother more. That was when she forced me into a room in the basement, where the screams were so loud they drowned out even the harshest of storms. I became a servant in my own home. But the obscurity of servitude kept me safe, away from her ice-cold eyes and away from whatever she did to make those people in the basement scream so loudly.

It was a dark, cold night when my curiosity got the best of me. Or perhaps it was my fear. Either way, I made the disastrous decision to follow those screams. I just couldn't take it anymore, bearing through every night the sounds of torture and pain.

So I got up and went to the door at the end of the hall. I pushed it open as quietly as I could. My eyes followed the sounds of agony that my ears had already been stalking.

That's when I saw my beautiful stepmother hovering over a table, dripping wet. The room resembled a dungeon, with chains hanging from the ceiling and strange-looking metal contraptions hiding in dark corners.

When my eyes got used to the darkness, I realized she wasn't just wet—she was covered in blood. The scarlet substance was everywhere: the table, the floor, all over her clothes and hands. But worse than that was a pulsating and dripping mass tightly gripped in her fingers.

My eyes darted to the right, and I gasped when I saw the half-naked man chained to the wall. A black hole gaped in his chest where his ribcage should have been sealed together.

The organ my stepmother was holding was his heart. She had cut his heart out.

Then she did the most appalling and frightening thing I have ever seen. She bent her head to the organ in her hands, and I realized suddenly why I had never seen her eat food before. My stepmother ate *hearts*.

I made a choked sound, and she heard me, snapping her head up at an impossible speed in my direction. Her lips dripped with blood that not a moment ago had pumped through the fleshy bulb in her hands.

I cried out when I noticed her face. My stepmother's beautiful, icy visage had transformed into a monstrous vision that I had only seen in my childhood nightmares. Her eyes shone a bright golden color, and her teeth gleamed sharply, covered in blood. She made a hissing sound, and that's when I finally snapped out of my stupor.

I ran away from the door and through the dark

hallways of the castle. I knew I had to get as far away from my stepmother as possible. I ran through the cold night until I had left the castle and its grounds behind. I ran until I reached the edge of the woods. I had always feared this place, and now I thought nothing of continuing forward.

Snow speckled the ground and the starless sky was patched with twisted tree branches, but even the dark unknown was less frightening to me than what I was running away from. I'm not sure how long I ran through the frigid forest. I just knew I could never go back. I knew the next time I saw her would be the death of me.

At some point during my race, I came upon a clearing. There was a small, stone cottage surrounded by a tall fence with an angry-looking gate. I slowed down and tried to catch my breath. I could hear dead tree branches knocking against rotted wooden shutters, and the sound of an owl hooting mixed with the howling of the wind. It was so cold that my lips and fingers had turned numb, and the snow had soaked right through my slippers. I knew if I stayed out in the forest all night, I would surely die, so I decided to take my chances with the house.

I walked through the creaky gate and approached the front door. Then I took a deep breath and summoned the last of my courage. Then I knocked.

There was no answer.

After knocking on the door three times and receiving no response, I figured no one was home. I tried the door and found it unlocked. In any normal circumstanc-es, I would never have entered a strange structure in the middle of the woods. But I was freezing and exhausted and had just about given up hope. It seemed that this abode was my last savior.

Inside, the cottage was dark. I could tell it had not been deserted, as it was filled with homey memorabilia. Dirty mugs littered the tabletop, and articles of clothing were haphazardly thrown about. I shut the door behind me and took a few steps inside. A menagerie of weapons lined the walls. Axes, swords, bow and arrows, wooden stakes, and more covered the room in a sort of morbid wallpaper. I shivered to myself.

Walking over to the fireplace, I noticed what seemed like a fresh pile of soot. I removed a log from the pile in the corner of the room and put it in the fireplace, us-ing the accompanying piece of flint to light the barest of flames. I carefully caressed the air around the flickering orange light until it became strong enough to survive on its own and provide me the warmth I so desperately needed.

As the heat from the fire slowly soaked into my chilled body, I grew tired. I lay down on the woven rug, pulling a nearby blanket on top of me. Within moments, I was fast asleep.

I awoke to a thundering noise as many sets of heavy footsteps stormed into the cottage. They gath-ered around me as my vision cleared enough for me to decipher who they were. Dwarves. There were seven of them. Each had a long beard, though the colors varied. Each was covered in dirt and grime. The sun had recently risen, its rays shooting through the open doorway behind them, making the small figures look almost angelic.

Somehow, they knew who I was before I could formally introduce myself. They had been foretold of my coming, or else they were not surprised to see me. They were more than hospitable, especially when they learned who I was running from. These dwarves were not just miners, although their excavation of precious gems did provide them a living. It turned out they were also Watchers. Their kind had been dedicated sentinels of the forest and the creatures within it.

They were more than familiar with my stepmother the queen. The one who seemed to be the leader of the group, the strongest of the dwarves with a salt-and-pepper beard, explained it to me in his deep voice. "Ever since she married your father, a darkness has come over the forest. Slowly but surely, her evil has been infecting the spirits of the woods. Servants are going missing from the nearby villages."

"She is evil, but what can I do to stop her?"

"You must kill her."

I was shocked to hear these harsh words and even more shocked that they didn't fully disgust me. "But how? I can't . . . I don't know how!"

"It's your duty and birthright to rescue your kingdom and restore safety to the realm."

"Maybe. Still, I cannot fight a monster like her."

They explained that they would teach me.

From the first dwarf, the leader, I began to learn about a world I had never even dreamed of. This was the world my stepmother came from, and its evil had threatened to strangle the last bit of life from my kingdom. Week by week, the first dwarf showed me old books, volumes of leather-bound yellow pages that explained and elaborated upon this darkness.

Once I had a good grasp of the knowledge, I needed to learn how to defeat the demoness who had usurped me. Three of the dwarves were experts in weaponry. They trained me on how to use a sword, a bow and arrow, and an ax. Where I once could barely nock an arrow, I could now shoot off three arrows with no time between them, hitting targets that seemed as far away as the horizon. Where I once could not spar with a sword for more than a minute without my lungs tiring, I now bested my opponents in fair matches. I strengthened my muscles and my mind, month after month, so I could wield these instruments of death without shaking and without uncertainty.

The fifth dwarf was quiet and reserved. He brought me into the forest and showed me the hidden souls of living things. He taught me how to recognize the rot that was encroaching upon the ecosystem. He instructed me in survival as well—which berries were safe to eat and how to avoid poisonous plants. From him, over the seasons, I learned not to fear the forest, but to worship it.

I was retaught my heritage by the sixth dwarf. He reminded me of who I was and where I'd come from. He knew everything about my father and the fathers who'd come before him. He re-instilled in me the deepest honor for my bloodline, one I had lost in the years of servitude to the villain who now ruled where I should.

The last dwarf was the most mysterious. He kept his distance for the most part until the rest of my training was complete. Then, one day, he bade me follow him, a twinkle in his eye. Quick as a sparrow, he flitted about the cottage, grabbing herbs and other ingredients that all went into the large iron kettle warming over the fire.

He tinkered with his potion for three days, as we went about our daily work and my continued training. Finally, it released bright green steam.

He gathered the others and pulled a shiny silver blade from his belt.

"Drinking this will help you defeat your stepmother. Set your intentions as you swallow, and it will imbue you with the stealth, wisdom, and power needed to make you a champion for your kingdom," he told me somberly. "Once you are ready, you will use the silver blade to cut out the demon's heart."

The leader nodded, and the others gathered around the fire. One by one, the dwarves stepped up to the kettle. Using the knife, each of them sliced their palm in turn, letting their own blood become an ingredient in the mysterious brew.

When it was ready, I dipped a copper mug into the

kettle, pulling it out nearly full of the dark red liquid. It was thick and warm and contained unidentifiable chunks as it slid down my throat, but I did not wince.

Where I once quivered at the shadows in the dark between trees, I would now relish the isolation the forest provided. I would no longer scan the woods for shining eyes, but march steadily onward, confident in my cause.

I turned to the group, my lips bright red from the blood that stained them, and spoke.

"It's time."

Personal Demons

It had started as a small, dark shadow in the corner of his eye, a shadow in his peripheral. It seemed a figure was following him home from the grocery store. Martin assumed it was just someone walking too closely at first, but before long, he realized that the figure was moving with him as if it was seared onto his eyeballs.

It quickly took shape and became three-dimensional before he was able to reach the safety of his own apartment. It looked like a monster from an old creature feature or an illustration from the Bible of the things that live in Hell.

When the creature had first started appearing to Martin, he could shake it off right away, but soon, the red glowing eyes became as much of a constant in his life as the deep knowledge that he could die any day.

Before he could figure out what to do about it— if he was going to do anything—the apparition had begun speaking to him. Any time he heard that deep, growling voice, the bottom of his stomach dropped out, and he had to use every ounce of his willpower to pretend it wasn't happening.

Eventually, Martin was seeing the demon every day in some form or another, and it became more and more difficult to ignore. Being an artist, Martin had done the only thing he could: he'd started sculpting it.

Martin was working the clay through his hands. He found solace in the comforting feeling of the cold, slimy material. Martin was a gifted sculptor. He'd had work featured in various museums on the East Coast and even a few out in California. He had been poised to be a breakout star in the art world—until the diagnosis brought his world crashing down.

Martin Edison was going to die soon.

Four months before, he'd been diagnosed with a brain tumor. An "inoperable malignant intracranial tumor," to be exact. After explaining that his body had created a bunch of cells that were strangling his brain, the doctor had told Martin he had only a couple of months left to live. He already felt like he was surviving on borrowed time.

Martin was spending more and more time isolated in his studio. The space felt like home to him; he was comforted by the familiar high ceilings and wood-paneled walls. The cement floor provided him a hassle-free clean-up, and the kiln in the corner reminded him to keep creating. Although his lease on the place was for another seven months, Martin thought to himself that the last few of them would see the place entirely empty.

He looked down at the figure forming on the table. It was a demon with cracked skin and thick, curved horns. Martin was becoming increasingly familiar with this image as it continued to encroach on his mind. The doctor had warned that the tumor would give him hallucinations. He hadn't warned him that those hallucinations might take the form of a fire-breathing creature from Hell.

Working his thumb over the sculpture of the creature, Martin smoothed down an area he wanted to re-texturize. Ironically, the demon that haunted him had also become his biggest source of inspiration. His studio was overflowing with statues of the beast in every shape and size: full-bodied to bust, small to large.

"Let me out, Martin," the demon's scratchy voice called from inside his head.

Martin tried to disregard what he knew was only a vicious side effect of his tumor. He continued working in silence, ignoring the voice even as his hands shook.

"Let me out, Martin," it repeated, stronger and more demanding.

Martin attempted again to ignore the voice. He focused on the clay figurine taking shape in front of him and not the demonic noise echoing in his skull.

All of a sudden, the mouth of the figure in his hands moved, and a deep voice thundered from it, "Let me OUT, Martin!"

Martin dropped the clay on the floor and sprung up. His heart was racing. He tried to calm down by reminding himself that it wasn't real, merely a waking nightmare.

Sighing, Martin picked up the clay; it was ruined, and he needed to start over. He dumped the wet glob in the bucket of overflow material and walked to his desk, a long table on the other side of his studio. Passing over the piles of papers and outdated desktop, Martin picked up a bottle of scotch and took a swig. He felt the hairs on the back of his neck prickle.

Turning around sharply, Martin gasped. Standing in front of him was the demon in the flesh. He'd seen it before, of course, but it had never been this *real* looking. Its skin was scaly, and its shadow filled the floor. A rotten odor drifted toward Martin. The beast stood ten feet tall with glowing red eyes and made a reptilian sound as it scanned the room.

"It's not real," Martin recited to himself, closing his eyes and trying to breathe through his latest hallucination. He opened one eye, but it was still there. He shut it quickly, shaking in the darkness of his eyelids.

"Let me out, Martin," the demon rumbled at him, the sound reverberating off the high ceiling.

This can't be happening. This isn't real. The overwhelming scent of sulfur contradicted his rational thoughts.

Martin took deep inhales, trying to overpower the mass on his brain making him hallucinate. Trembling, he turned away from the demon and walked back to his desk, as if he weren't seeing the spawn of Satan in his work studio.

His hands shaking, Martin picked up a small bust from the desk and walked over to the kiln. The demon's presence was heavy behind him, looming like an oncoming storm. Martin pulled the heavy door open and stepped inside, placing the bust on the shelf. He could hear the snorts from the imaginary demon. He felt its presence as much as he knew it didn't exist. Trying to ignore the hallucination, he moved the rest of the unfinished pieces into the kiln, shut the door, and turned the power on, watching as the orange light indicated the temperature rising inside.

Having nothing left to distract himself from his mind's tricks, Martin turned once more toward the demon. He gasped as the towering monster strode up, stopping within a few inches of him. Martin shook with terror, thinking for the first time that this creature was too real. He could feel its warm breath, smell its rotten egg odor, and see the red glow from its eyes.

Maybe this isn't a hallucination after all. Maybe this is a real demon.

It started laughing then, increasing in volume and intensity until its thunderous roar echoed through the studio. As it shook with amusement, plumes of smoke rose off its body.

"Let me OUT, MARTIN," the demon demanded, his voice creating the most spine-tingling feeling Martin had ever experienced.

Martin froze in fear, unsure if what he was seeing was a figment of his medically-induced imagination, or if maybe—just maybe—there was a demon standing in front of him.

The creature locked eyes with Martin and inched

forward at a tortuously slow pace. Thinking quickly, Martin scanned the room for an escape. The door was too far; he would never make it past the hulking figure in front of him to get there in time.

He turned instead toward the kiln. Trapping the demon in there might be his only way to escape its wrath. It was worth a shot. If two thousand degrees Fahrenheit couldn't kill this thing, nothing could.

Martin backed up toward the kiln. His legs moved as if through a viscous fluid as the monster painstakingly followed his every step. The demon's glowing red eyes bore into Martin's skull through the layers of skin and bone and into the cancerous cells themselves.

Finally, Martin reached the oven. He put his hand behind him, not taking his eyes off the demon that continued to take slight steps toward him. Martin resisted the urge to scream, having accepted the idea that this was indeed a real-life monster and not something he was hallucinating.

Quickly, he yanked the door open without looking at it. His plan seemed to be working as the demon lunged toward him, and he made a move to shoot sideways out of the way.

But a piece of wet clay on the floor caused him to trip backward. At that same moment, the demon made contact, falling on top of Martin on the floor of the kiln. The heavy door slammed closed behind them, and the heat from the large oven enveloped Martin. Death consumed them both.

Days later, the police found the charred body of Martin Edison inside the kiln. The incident was officially declared an accident. His friends and family knew Martin had been suffering from depression, even delusions, because of his diagnosis. They had all spoken about how he was becoming something of a recluse, hiding away in his studio and pulling back from the outside world. None of them were shocked when they heard the news, many believing his death to have been self-inflicted.

There were no signs of anyone else having been in the studio that night, and the door was locked from the inside. No fingerprints graced the door of the kiln except Martin's own. In fact, the on-site coroner had noticed nothing out of the ordinary, save for an unexplainable smell of sulfur.

Consume

am Cronos; I am Saturn, Ruler of the Titans and God of Time. I am the strongest being to grace this universe, stronger even than my father, Uranus, whom I overthrew with a sickle, tossing his manhood into the raging sea. Who would dare challenge me, the product of the earth and sky, the holy lord, and supreme leader of this realm? I am the King of Kings. I am the master of this land and all above and all below. To defy me is to decry the cosmos itself.

As I overthrew my own father, prophecy warned me that I, too, would become a story of patricide. By my own child, my own shame. I could not allow that to happen. To survive and keep hold of my power, I knew I must become a destructive, all-devouring force.

My sister-wife Rhea bore me many children, but I could not suffer them to live, not if I wanted to ensure my reign. After each child was born, I swallowed them in turn: modest Hestia, fertile Demeter, dark Hades, saline Poseidon, regal Hera. I reveled in their consumption, their masses sliding down my slippery gullet. Stabs of pain like electricity pricked my esophagus, intermingling with shudders of pleasure at the power I had to crush these would-be usurpers.

But Rhea the lioness betrayed me. She stowed away

her youngest born, the thunder god Zeus, on Krete. Shield-clashing Kouretes guarded the babe as she conspired against me with wise Metis. She wrapped an imposter in a golden blanket and presented it to me as her son. In my haste—and my cockiness—I swallowed the package without inspecting it first. Absorbed in my victory, I did not note the object's strange taste, its inflexibility as it made its way past my pharynx.

Then there were the tastes of mustard and wine. Soon I was overcome with the desperate need to purge my body of its contents. I tore at the flesh on my abdomen until my fingernails came away with blood and skin. I felt the mass rising upward, choking me from the inside. I was regurgitating something heavy and harmful. It was a massive stone, gray under a bloody bile layer, knocking out my teeth, tearing away the flesh around my mouth. Then all six of my consumed brood erupted from my body.

Hence Zeus of thunder made his move to free his siblings from their intestinal confines. He had masqueraded as a cupbearer to deceive me, and now that the deed was done, my seven offspring sought revenge. They allied with my enemies—the Hecatonchires and the Cyclopes—in their rebellion.

For ten years, we battled. We were pelted with stones, struck by lightning, deafened by thunder. I fought alongside my brethren: Atlas, Hyperion, Theia, Oceanus, and Themis. We were great, and we were many, but we could not beat back the combined strength of my children and their confederates. My progeny overtook our forces; the prophecy had been fulfilled.

Ever since, I have been a prisoner, languishing in the pit of Tartarus far beneath Hades. Here in the dark abyss, I wait for the day when I will once again rise to rule. I see in my future the Elysian Islands, home of the blessed dead. I am Cronos; I am Saturn, Ruler of the Titans and God of Time.

The Abandoned Princess

Once upon a time, there was a kingdom divided in two. In the center was the royal citadel. Beautiful courtyard gardens connected tall towers made from shining stones that comprised the royal palace. Around this was the imposing city wall that separated the luxurious inner lifestyles from the hellish world outside.

The people outside the walls lived in darkness and filth, scrounging for food in a world where danger awaited them at every turn. Crime was rampant, and the laws were rarely enforced. This world seemed awash in a gray palette, and smiles were harder to come by than spare coins.

While everything was dark outside the walls, those inside the citadel lived in blissful ignorance. In the highest of the palace towers lived the king and queen and their favorite courtiers. The couple had been married ten years before, during the Year of the Crow. They had been advised by the royal seers not to rush their union, to wait for the stars to align, but in haste, they'd moved quickly forward anyway. Everyone in the citadel celebrated the nuptials for ten days and ten nights. The new king and queen prayed for many sons to carry on their legacy.

Unfortunately, that was not to be; the queen did not give birth to any sons. Instead, the couple had six daughters, each more beautiful than the next. One year, the queen declared that the child growing in her belly would be her last. They hoped for a boy but were dismayed when she delivered a rosy-cheeked female instead. Still, they resolved to love their little disappointment, so long as she fell in line with the rest of her siblings.

But Bellamy was different from her sisters. Where the others adored spending hours combing their hair and trying on jewels, she despised wearing finery and lounging around. She yearned for the outside world and adventure, things that were forbidden. Members of the royal family never left the citadel's safety for the outside world of death and decay. Still, Bellamy itched to see beyond the stone walls that surrounded her.

While her sisters batted eyelashes at lords, Bellamy showed no interest in any of the men. In fact, the only person in the entire palace who had turned her head was a serving girl named Violet. She was Bellamy's same age and more beautiful than any precious stone. Violet's smile lit up the cold winter nights, and her laugh danced like a melody on the wind. Bellamy was smitten.

One day, Bellamy's parents caught her kissing Violet. Her mother cursed her, and her father banished her from the royal tower. Her sisters laughed and pulled at Bellamy's hair, crying that if she would act like a boy, she should look like one too. Ragged and torn apart, the young princess was forced away from her family's velvet-lined walls and through the royal corridors. From that day forward, she was officially abandoned by the king and queen.

Before she was cast out entirely, Bellamy's grandparents took her in. They secreted her among their rooms in the westernmost tower of the palace, far enough that her parents did not know she still lived within the walls. There she lived peacefully for a few years, reading books and dreaming of what existed beyond her reach.

One day, there was a knock at the door. Two figures entered the room, their faces obscured by red velvet capes; it was the king and queen. Each was pale and haggard and wore dark circles under their eyes. They were but sickly shadows of the reigning couple Bellamy remembered from her childhood.

"Daughter, we need your help," they pleaded.

She stayed silent and immobile, wondering how they had found her.

"We are both ill! The doctors can't fix it. They've tried everything. The seers have told us there is a cure, but it lies far outside the citadel's walls. We can't trust any of the servants and have pleaded with your sisters, but none of them will go beyond the walls. We need your help. Please."

Bellamy's stomach fluttered. Although she held no affection for her neglectful parents, she recognized this as an opportunity for adventure. She nodded and said, "I will go outside of the walls. I will venture into the underworld to save you."

Adorning herself in men's clothing and covering her recently shorn-off hair with a shabby cap, Bellamy left the tower and her family's tears. At the gate, she faltered, her fear almost overcoming her. With resolve, she stepped into a world of darkness and left the safety of the citadel behind.

Bellamy knew she could not trust just anyone. She spent days slinking around stone walls wet with dirty rain, eating meager bits of taffy, and sleeping rough when she needed rest. She avoided unsavory characters by keeping to the shadows, searching with her head down. She had heard whispers of an apothecary run by a mysterious woman who could cure even the rarest of diseases.

After six days, Bellamy found a small shop tucked into a corner. The sign was small, but its symbols told her she had found the right place. She knocked on the door. The woman who answered was tall and somber with dark, shining eyes.

Before she could speak, Bellamy was ushered inside and guided to a table, where she ate dark stew and grainy bread. She told her story in between bites while the mysterious woman stared silently.

"I will help you. But first, I will teach you," the woman said at last. She introduced herself as Muriel and immediately took up at her workbench, mixing herbs and ingredients so fast Bellamy's eyes could barely keep up.

Bellamy lived with Muriel for three weeks. She learned from the woman how to create consequences from resources. Bellamy cooked three meals a day and slept in front of the hearth at night.

Late one evening, after the two women had sat together in comfortable silence for hours in front of the warm fire, Muriel invited Bellamy into her bed. She spent every night after there.

Forgetting about the citadel and her sick parents, Bellamy's thoughts were thenceforth only for Muriel and the craft. Her hands took up potions like a second nature, and each day she soaked up knowledge as a sea sponge would salty water.

One night, while lying in each other's arms under the thick, colorful quilts that adorned the feather mattress, Bellamy asked Muriel about the potion to save her parents, the king and queen.

"And do you want to save them, these parents who so readily abandoned you?" Muriel asked, looking deeply into Bellamy's eyes.

Bellamy hesitated briefly before curling closer to her love. "Yes, I do."

Muriel kissed her and nodded solemnly.

The next day, they began collecting ingredients. After another six days of carefully obtaining, measuring, and combining a plethora of rare materials, it was complete. In the pot splashed a shimmering cerulean liquid. Muriel carefully poured the viscous substance into a teardrop-shaped vial, stopping it with a cork.

Donning a cloak of midnight black, Bellamy left Muriel's abode. Her heart ached at leaving what had become home to her. She made her way through the labyrinth of dirty streets, stepping over piles of waste and bodies caught between sleep and death. She eventually reached the massive wooden gates of the citadel.

Calling up to the guards, Bellamy demanded entrance. Only after she showed her face did they recognize her as a member of the royal family and allow her to cross the threshold from grime to opulence.

Once inside, Bellamy made her way to the tallest tower, fighting back memories of the day she had been cast out by the very people she had come to save. Crows circled overhead, and the courtyards were oddly quiet. A strange sense of foreboding seemed to hang in the air. Bellamy made her way to the center of the citadel and finally up the center tower's stairs to the royal couple's bedroom.

On soft burgundy bedsheets lay her parents, their bodies as cold and stiff as corpses. She crept up cautiously, uncorking the potion bottom. Carefully, Bellamy tipped the liquid into her mother's mouth, then her father's. She waited seconds that felt like hours.

With a gasp, both monarchs awoke. The color flushed back into their cheeks as they became warm-blooded again.

"Our daughter! You have saved us! You have done what no one else would do!" They embraced her. "Please, come home; we will re-establish you as a princess of the royal court and make you heir to the throne!"

Bellamy was quiet. She looked around at the finery-draped walls but saw only a cage that housed her body but not her mind.

"Thank you, Mother and Father. I am honored to have brought you back from the brink. But I cannot stay. No, I must go where my heart is."

Then she turned and walked out of the tower, away from the citadel, and back to her new life.

The Crukker

"There's never any service out here," Ellie complained, waving her cellphone in all directions, trying to get a signal. Her face was painted with whiskers, and cat ears topped her light-brown hair.

"It's the Pine Barrens! What do you expect?" answered Bryan from the passenger seat. His boyfriend, James, laughed and grabbed his shoulder from behind. James, Chad, Nafessa, and Ellie were squished into the backseat, with Ellie pretty much spread out across everyone's laps. It hadn't been easy fitting six college students into a four-door sedan.

The group of friends was driving down a dark road in southern New Jersey on Halloween night. Their original plan had been to go to the haunted hayride earlier, around 8 p.m., and then make it back up to campus in time to hit their friend Jake's Halloween bash. Unfortunately, Ellie had gotten held up at her sorority's trick-or-treating event, and Chad had somehow lost his keys to his apartment. They hadn't ended up hitting the road until closer to 9:30 p.m.

"Well, we would be on the hayride by now if everyone had their shit together," Austin complained from the driver's seat. He was dressed as a "mad doctor," complete with fake blood spatters and a plastic stethoscope. Bryan had helped create some fake wounds on his face using liquid latex.

They were coming from Rutgers University, and the drive was only a little over an hour long, but Ellie insisted they stop to pee about halfway down.

"I bet they only have porta-potties there, and no thank you," she said as they got back in the car. "Plus, you got your pork roll, egg, and cheese sandwich, so stop complaining."

"Yeah, I'm never going to be mad about stopping at Wawa," Nafessa chimed in, sipping on her iced coffee. The Long Islander had only been introduced to the mid-Atlantic staple convenience store since she'd enrolled in the university, but like the rest of them, she had quickly become obsessed.

"You said it," Chad echoed, his mouth still full of hoagie. He wiped crumbs off the bandana tied around his neck and took a chug from his Gatorade bottle. Chad and Austin had met in a business class and tried dating some nine months ago. While they'd realized it wasn't a match made in heaven, they remained friends with occasional benefits.

The car turned off the main road and down an even darker street lined with thick coniferous trees.

"I heard there are homeless mental patients who wander around down here," teased Chad.

"Oh, please," Ellie chuckled. "You're just scared because you've never been south of Mercer County!"

They all laughed at that. Austin and Bryan had been best friends for many years, growing up together down in South Jersey. When Bryan had met Ellie at school—she was pre-vet and he was studying agricultural science, so they'd been assigned to the same dorm freshman year—the three of them had become nearly inseparable.

A few minutes later, Nafessa and Chad were talking about the guy in the Wawa parking lot who had incorrectly identified her Halloween costume.

"He asked me if I was dressed as Beyoncé. Do people not know who Rosie the Riveter is?" As a history major, Nafessa was always using the holiday to dress as her favorite historical figures. Last year she'd been Maya Angelou, and the year before that she'd been Frida Kahlo.

"Aw babe, don't worry; your costume is iconic," Ellie assured her girlfriend. They'd been dating for about three months now, and Nafessa had luckily fit in seamlessly with Ellie's friends.

They spotted the giant homemade arrow pointing people toward the fairgrounds, and Austin turned the car into the gravel parking lot. The group nearly fell out of the doors, thankful to be free of their confinement. They stretched their sore limbs and made their way to the ticket booth, walking past an overstuffed scarecrow dressed in flannel that screamed "Brooklyn hipster" rather than "rural farmer."

"Hey Ellie, look, it's your ex-boyfriend!" Bryan

teased, pointing at the scarecrow. He was referring to the frat boy she had very briefly dated a year before.

Ellie rolled her eyes, laughing nervously. She gave Nafessa a side-glance, hoping her girlfriend wasn't bothered by the comment. Luckily, Nafessa seemed too distracted by the preteens screaming and running around on the other side of the parking lot.

"Go Titans!" someone shouted at the group as they walked through the grounds.

James hooted back, happy that someone acknowledged his Marcus Mariota costume. He admired the Hawaiian football player because of their shared heritage and shared passion for pigskin. James and Bryan had been dating for almost a year now. The engineering major had met the redhead at a meeting of the school's gay-straight alliance. They'd been together ever since.

Nodding at the rows of corn surrounding the perimeter of the event space, Austin turned to Bryan and said, "I thought they couldn't grow crops in the Barrens."

"They can't, mostly. The soil is too acidic. This area here is a bit different from down the road, though." Bryan pointed toward the horizon, past the cornfield and the paved road that edged around it. "See the tree line? That's where the Barrens start technically." As an agriculture major and a lifelong resident of the Garden State, Bryan knew a lot about the natural resources of New Jersey. He had always been especially fascinated by the history of the Pine Barrens.

"We took a tour of the cranberry bogs last year,"

James said, putting his arm around Bryan. "We watched them corral the berries in the water using these giant shovel-looking tools. It was pretty neat."

There was a large handmade display positioned near the ticket booth with the words "Horrors of New Jersey" scrawled across the top in red paint that was meant to look like blood, presumably. The famous Jersey Devil was front and center, surrounded by other creepy topics like "Ghosts of Asbury Park," "The Devil's Tree," and "Camp Pahaquarry." In the bottom left corner was a crude drawing of a man in waders with "The Crukker" scrawled atop it.

"Have you guys heard of the Crukker?" Austin teased in his best Vincent Price voice.

"No, what is it?" asked Nafeesa.

Bryan and Ellie rolled their eyes; they clearly knew the story already.

"Okay, Piney boy, tell us the story," Chad retorted, even though he was familiar with the story.

"The Crukker is a local legend," Austin began in a hushed voice. "Supposedly he works the bogs, but in his spare time, he likes to murder children. They say he lures his victims in with soda and candy. Late at night, you can still hear their cries."

"Good thing we're not children!" Nafessa said.

"Hey, speak for yourself!" Chad replied with a fake Western accent, tipping his cowboy hat and making the others laugh.

"Ellie is basically the size of a child!" Bryan teased

his five-foot-two best friend, who replied by sticking her tongue out at him. "I heard it differently. Where I'm from, they say the Crukker is a grouchy man who lives in the cranberry bogs and kills anyone who trespasses on his land."

"See, now, I thought he was a mental patient who went around South Jersey murdering people randomly," Ellie said.

The group laughed at the disparities between the versions of the urban legend.

They reached the ticket booth only to find that the haunted hayride was sold out. It was already past 11 p.m., and the only thing left for them to buy tickets for was the flashlight corn maze.

James turned back to the group with a "Well, what do you think?" look, and, after some encouraging nods, he bought six tickets.

The air was getting colder, and Bryan was glad he'd grabbed his zip-up hoodie. He knew his slutty eighties summer camp counselor costume would be a hit at the party later tonight, but perhaps it wasn't entirely practical for a romp through the cornfield. Shrugging, he followed the group toward the rear of the Fall Festival, where the entrance to the cornfield was.

The sounds of terrified teenagers and buzzing chainsaws fell away as the group reached the dark entrance to the maze. They were handed three flashlights and a walkie-talkie to use to contact the staff in case they got lost. The young woman who took their tickets warned them that the event closed at midnight, so they needed to be out by then.

Together, they made their way into the rows of corn. No one noticed the dark figure peering out at them from along the stalks.

The group let the beams from their flashlights guide them around corners and down dirt paths, laughing when they came upon a dead end and had to turn around. As they made their way back down a now-rejected path, Bryan saw something move in his peripheral. He turned his head quickly, the flashlight beam following. No one was there. He shrugged, figuring his imagination was playing tricks on him in the darkness.

Some ten minutes later, the group of friends was laughing together over one of Chad's jokes when a distinct rustling sound came from the stalks in front of them. Everyone paused at once. No one said anything.

"Did you guys hear that?" asked Nafeesa.

James stepped up to the corn, feeling the stalks to confirm they were bent in the area where the sound had come from.

"Someone was definitely walking through here," he said to the group.

Ellie shivered, and Chad shone his flashlight around in circles.

"Whoever they are, they're gone now," Austin commented.

The friends continued down the path, a bit quieter and more hesitant than they had been before.

Eventually, the wrong turns stopped being funny and started being frustrating. The minutes were ticking by, and the group seemed to have not gotten that far at all. Still, the adventurous Halloween spirit pushed them forward.

Ellie was at the front of the line this time. She took her phone out to check the time and in doing so also took her eyes off the path in front of her.

"Oomph," she let out as she bumped into something solid. "Hey, why'd you stop?" she asked, forgetting that all her friends were behind her.

Slowly, Ellie's eyes moved up the hulking silhouette in front of her. She was about to speak again when the figure lifted its arm and swiped at her, slashing at the inside of her arm with an unidentifiable weapon.

Ellie let out a scream, and the rest of the group rushed forward—but by the time anyone thought to look up in the direction she was frantically pointing in, there was nothing there. The evidence remained, however, in the dark flow of blood coming from the inside of her elbow.

"Shit, it's close to the brachial artery," she said.

Quickly, Bryan took the yellow sweatband off his head and wrapped it around his best friend's arm above the slice. Then he took off his hoodie and pressed down firmly on the wound. He had been a lifeguard for the previous few summers and was silently thanking his first-aid training for kicking in. Nafessa comforted her girlfriend by smoothing her hair and whispering to her that everything would be okay.

Meanwhile, Austin and James ran forward, looking for Ellie's mystery attacker. They both returned to the huddled group a few moments later, panting.

"We couldn't find anyone," Austin said.

James's jaw was set with determination, but fear still seeped through his eyes.

"It could just be some dumb kids playing a prank," Bryan said hopefully.

"Pretty fucked-up prank," Nafeesa muttered under her breath.

"Where's Chad?" Austin burst out.

Everyone looked shocked, and no one could remember where he had gone or when he'd left.

"Chad?" Austin began shouting. "Chad!" He rushed from corner to corner, unable to spot anyone around. James and Bryan started doing the same.

Nafeesa carefully helped Ellie stand up, continuing to apply pressure to her wound. Bryan's hoodie had turned from blue to red.

Suddenly, the bright lights in the distance cut out. The night was entirely dark.

"Shit," Nafeesa said, looking at her phone. "It's midnight. They're closing down."

"They can't leave us in here!" Ellie screeched.

"Call that woman, tell her we need help," Bryan suggested.

Austin turned to him, pale. "Chad had the walkie talkie."

"Fuck," James exclaimed.

Ellie let out a half-sob. Nafeesa took a deep breath, turning to the group. "Okay, everyone, let's stay calm. We have two flashlights. We know there is an exit to this maze. We also know the main road is nearby. We need to find Chad and get out of here and get Ellie some medical attention."

"What about the psycho with the knife?" Bryan asked.

Everyone looked scared, as if the reality of danger was sitting heavily on the air above them, pressing down. The atmosphere was electric and prickled with tension.

"This is ridiculous," Ellie whispered. "How far do you think we've made it through the maze?"

They turned in circles, shining their remaining two lights at the stalks of corn that looked the same in every direction.

"I have no idea," Nafeesa said.

At the same time, Bryan guessed, "I think we're about halfway through, somewhere in the middle."

"Should we split up?" James asked.

"No!" Ellie shouted. "That's a terrible idea. There's a crazy man who tried to gut me!"

"Okay, okay, let's stop and think," Bryan said, trying to maintain calm. "The exit to the maze is near the parking lot. James, Ellie, and I will go on forward and try to get Ellie to a car so we can get her to a hospital. Austin and Nafeesa, you guys try to retrace your steps. See if you can find Chad or make it back to the beginning and flag down someone for help. Does anyone have service?"

They all shook their heads, already knowing their phones would be of no use.

"I'm not leaving you," Nafeesa said to her girlfriend.

"It's okay, babe," said Ellie. "I'll be okay. Bryan knows first aid. You and Austin are the fastest; you'll get back in time to get help. I'll be okay." She held Nafeesa close and kissed her before breaking apart with her half of the group.

Nafeesa and Austin started back down the way they came at a speed that was between walking and running. The sound of the wind through the stalks was louder than expected, and they often mistook it for the sound of someone walking in their direction.

"This is crazy, right?" Nafessa asked in a loud whisper. "Why is there someone out here with a weapon attacking random people?"

"Definitely not normal and NOT okay," Austin replied.

Suddenly a shadow blocked out the beam of the flashlight. Ahead of them was a hulking figure dressed in chest-high rubber waders. He held a long, flat metal instrument that resembled a thin, albeit sharp, shovel.

Before they had a chance to scream, the figure moved, and Austin's head was cleanly sliced off his body.

Nafeesa froze in panic at the sight of spurting blood coming from the stump of his neck. When his body hit the ground, it spurred her into motion. Unfortunately, it was too late.

As she turned to run, the large man was nearly on top of her. The two of them fell back into the rigid stalks of corn, landing hard in the dirt. Nafeesa shouted for help and then screamed in pain as the villain stabbed her over and over again through her abdomen. She only stopped shouting when the blood clogged her windpipe, overflowing from her lips. Then, she was still.

Bryan, Ellie, and James were desperately trying to find their way through the maze toward the parking lot. In the quiet, something cracked beneath James's foot. He looked down and spotted an old glass Coca-Cola bottle.

Before he could register it, his head snapped up at the sound of screaming across the cornfield. The horrified noises sounded frantic, but they couldn't figure out what direction they were coming from. Never-ending rows of corn obscured the sounds' direction, making them impossible to follow.

"Nafeesa!" Ellie shrieked.

James turned to her. "I'll help them; you two keep going!"

Before Bryan or Ellie could protest, the man was off running once again toward what he believed to be the center of the cornfield. Ellie let out a strangled moan of frustration, but Bryan, working on pure adrenaline at this point, pulled her forward. Together, they made their way through the dark, stumbling over broken corn stalks and wincing at every noise that made its way through the crops to their ears.

"Why did he have to run off on his own? Stupid James, always being the hero," Bryan was mumbling to himself.

"Do you think they're okay?" Ellie asked anxiously.

Bryan didn't respond because he honestly had no idea. Abruptly, his foot made contact with something peeking out from the bottom of the stalks. He looked down, and as his eyes adjusted, he realized with horror that it was a body.

"Oh my god, Chad!" Ellie yelped.

Bryan too recognized the face, even though half of it was missing. He pulled Ellie in the opposite direction, turning right at the fork in front of them,

"We have to get out of here; come on!"

They ran, turning this way and that without any strategy. Suddenly, Bryan collided with another body, realizing right before his heart jumped out of his body that it was James. His boyfriend looked terrified.

"It's the Crukker!" James shouted. "I saw him; he's dressed like a cranberry harvester!" James's announcement may have been funny if the other two hadn't just stumbled across their friend's corpse.

James opened his mouth to say something else, but before any words could leave his lips, his eyes went wide. A shadow moved behind him as his body fell face-first to the ground, a sharp instrument sticking out from the back of his head. Ellie screamed.

For a moment, Bryan froze. All sound seemed to fade away, and the only thing he could focus on was the dead body of the man he loved. He willed his limbs to move, to go to him, but deep down he knew there was no saving James. Hoping he'd have time to be heartbroken later, Bryan allowed his instincts to kick in.

Together, the two best friends took off running once more. Ellie was sobbing, making it difficult for her to breathe and slowing them down. Bryan kept pulling her forward until they turned left and smacked into another dead end.

Whirling around to go back, they saw the Crukker blocking the path not fifteen feet away.

Bryan moved in front of Ellie to protect her, but tripped and tilted sideways into the stalks, breaking them as he fell. The figure descended on his best friend, stabbing her in the gut and pulling the weapon upward. The blade and Ellie's body lifted into the air. The figure shoved the girl to the side, and she landed in a heap of limbs and guts.

Without giving himself time to react to yet another loss, Bryan raced through the rows of corn, the stiff stalks leaving small cuts on his bare arms and legs. He ran until his lungs would surely burst, but he could hear the sounds of heavy footsteps gaining on him.

All of a sudden, he was pushed onto the ground. The

Crukker landed on top of him, but his weapon skidded off to the right.

Bryan struggled to get out from under the heavy weight that pinned him to the dirt. For a brief moment, he looked up and saw the night sky full of stars. Then the Crukker moved on top of him, and Bryan jumped into action, pushing away from the stocky killer and trying to escape his grasp. Now without his weapon, the Crukker was trying to get his thick hands around Bryan's throat.

Looking to the right, Bryan saw the Crukker's discarded cranberry rake lying a few feet away.

He reached out, stretching his fingers to their physical limit. Frustrated as they merely brushed against the weapon, Bryan took a deep breath and heaved himself toward the makeshift weapon, managing to finally grasp it in his hand. In one last burst of energy, he swung his upper body off the ground while thrusting out with the metal rake.

The Crukker lunged forward as the instrument met with his face, slicing diagonally across his brow, nose, and cheeks and embedding itself in his flesh. Blood spurted out from the man's face as he fell to the ground, immobile.

Bryan carefully stood up, not taking his eyes off the still figure on the ground. Backing away slowly, he realized that he was unarmed.

Bryan bent down to grasp the handle of the rake, yanking it out from where it rested inside the killer's face. The flesh made a squishing sound and blood oozed out from the wound as the tool came free.

Bryan stared at the body on the ground, his vision becoming red as he registered that this man—thing—whatever—had killed his friends and his boyfriend. With a cry, he raised the rake in the air and brought it down right onto the Crukker's face once more.

Orca

I have the best job in the world. I work with orca whales at Ocean Planet, a top-rated waterpark and aquarium in sunny Florida. Of all the people who work here, and all the animals they train, I'm considered the most elite because I get to work with the flagship species. Whenever you see a commercial for Ocean Planet, you see orcas, and sometimes specifically my orca: Makana.

"Hi, Gale, how are you?" I address one of the older ticket ladies. She waves and continues counting the cash in her drawer as I walk through the employees-only entrance. I love getting to know all the employees here, especially knowing I hold probably the most coveted position in the park. I'm kind of like a mini-celebrity in that way.

I smile to myself as I make my way through the park, passing seals and penguins on my route to the kitchens. Every morning, I stop here to grab a bucket of fresh (and incredibly stinky) fish, which I use to encourage positive behavior in my whale friend. When she performs a trick correctly, she gets a herring or a mackerel. This is how she knows I love her and support her. We have a bond that no one else could possibly understand.

I can hear the protesters' faint shouts outside the

park's far wall. I roll my eyes, imagining those misinformed hippies wasting their time chanting and stomping around in the sun. They like to make a fuss about the whales being kept in captivity because they think it's "unnatural" and "unfair."

I've heard all their protestations before, and ever since the documentary aired, there's been a surge in unnecessary hate toward Ocean Planet. We do a lot of great conservation work here, but all people want to talk about is how the whales shouldn't be doing tricks. These are incredibly smart animals; they like doing tricks and getting tasty rewards. People are so quick to jump to conclusions about things they know nothing about.

What those protesters don't understand is that I genuinely love Makana. I care for her in the best way possible. She gets regular meals and doctor visits, protection from outside threats, and love and affection from myself. Whales in captivity even live longer than those in the wild!

After collecting the bucket of chum, I enter the underground tunnels that allow staff to walk around unbothered by visitors. After a few twists and turns and passing janitors, construction crew, and other animal trainers, I come to the stairs leading to the orca enclosure. They're doing work on some of the light fixtures outside the enclosure, making my job more difficult. Don't they know how important it is that I stick to Makana's schedule?

Stepping around half a dozen orange construction

cones set up by the electricians, I make my way around the outside of the tank and toward the staff entrance door. I step inside the office where I record all my work with Makana, looking for my clipboard.

Bzzzzzt.

Puzzled, I turn to confront this strange sound only to see a live wire flying toward my face, electricity buzzing off in sparks. Before I have time to move out of the way or even scream, I feel my body hum with voltage, and then everything goes dark.

When I regain consciousness, I can't see clearly; everything is out of focus. It feels like my senses were restarted like a computer and are slowly coming back online. I know I must have fallen to the ground after being electrocuted, but I don't feel any hard concrete underneath me. Has someone moved me?

I realize with a start that I am not on the ground or any other solid surface; I am under water. Where I once felt the reach of ten digits, I now have awkward fins. Instead of splitting into two independent limbs, my lower half is welded together. I feel simultaneously sleek and cumbersome, unused to my new form yet possessing an unconscious ability to use it.

Behind the wall of confusion and panic in my mind, a light of understanding appears. At first small, it soon grows until I finally understand what happened with a great heaviness. Somehow, I am an orca whale—or at least I am myself but inside of an orca—and not just any whale, but my beloved Makana. Alongside my own consciousness is something else, someone that is wholly Makana. I feel her emotions and remember her memories.

I can remember Makana's home, the cold waters swirling with the natural rhythms of the ocean. I can hear, see, and sense the rest of the pod around me. They were my mothers, sisters, aunts, children. They were my family. I ache with a longing to swim alongside them again. I want to click and clatter and breach with these beautiful beings who knew me before I was torn away from my home.

Upon realizing this, I shake with an unbearable wave of sadness and loss. The water in this tank is too warm, too clear, too dead. Compared to the vibrant vastness of the ocean, it is a stagnant pool that only serves to keep me locked up. I feel utterly hopeless and alone, isolated from anything I knew or loved. I am a prisoner.

The Devil Down in Jersey

It was a typical Pine Barrens landscape; the soil was sandy, the trees coniferous, and the insects and amphibians loud. A large, overturned tree trunk seemed to mark the beginning of a trail. A young woman placed a camera carefully on a rock, then walked toward the trunk and sat down on it. She wore hiking boots, shorts, and a T-shirt, her outfit topped off with a baseball cap. Clearing her throat, she began speaking directly to the camera, which was set up to face her.

"My name is Mia Brown. I'm a graduate student researching the traditions and folklore of New Jersey's Pine Barrens. I'm spending this weekend camping in the Barrens to get some on-the-ground experience and hopefully interview some local folks. This video is part of my application to the Richardson Grant Program. If awarded funding from the program, I'll be able to create a comprehensive database of local folklore and history from the Pine Barrens, preserving an important part of New Jersey's culture."

The woman looked awkwardly around, and then got up and walked over to turn off the camera. She got inside a red truck parked on the side of the road, starting the vehicle. She made a U-turn back onto the gravel road. The wheels churned up dirt, kicking it into the air.

Thick pitch pines lined the road.

Mia placed the camera on the dashboard, facing it toward her. She narrated while driving, "The Pinelands include over a million acres, making up twenty-two percent of New Jersey's landmass. This area is bigger than the Grand Canyon and Yosemite but less well-known across the country. In 1978, Congress designated it a natural reserve, and it was upgraded to an international biosphere reserve ten years later."

Swampy areas dotted the woods on either side of the road. The water was green and slimy, and insects skated on its oily surface. The sun shone through the windshield, illuminating smudges on the glass and creating a glare on the camera screen.

"The people who live down here are often referred to as 'Pineys,' and not necessarily in a good way. Since the colonization of New Jersey, they've often been poor and discriminated against, and there were even eugenics studies in the early nineteen-hundreds that condemned them. I want to make it clear that all the people I've talked to who live down here have been incredibly kind and helpful with my research."

The truck slowed and turned off onto another road, leaving the forest behind and passing carefully mowed fields edged by wooden fences. Mia pulled into a parking lot and turned off her car. She made her way to the building in front of her.

"We're at the Batsto Nature Center in Historic Batsto Village in Wharton State Forest, part of the Pinelands Nature Reserve and the largest state park in New Jersey. Batsto was a thriving village in the mid-nineteenth century, but it's now just a historical landmark sitting right here in the middle of the Pines."

Mia entered the building, ignored by the person with their head down at the welcome desk. Locating the entrance to an exhibit, she veered left, keeping her camera on and pointed forward.

As Mia walked through the room, she zoomed in on different objects: agricultural tools, old maps, black-and-white photographs. She approached a poster with a drawing of an odd-looking animal with the words WANTED: JERSEY DEVIL written across the top in an old-timey font. At the bottom, it offered a two-hundred-and-fifty-thousand-dollar reward and wanted readers to "approach with extreme caution."

Narrating again, Mia began, "Perhaps the most well-known legend of the Pine Barrens is that of the Jersey Devil. This mythological creature is said to have the head of a goat, wings of a bat, cloven hooves, and a forked tail. While many people chalk it up to mere mistaken identity, others argue that the creature's existence predates white colonization. Local Native Americans, the Lenni Lenape, sometimes referred to the Barrens as 'The Place of the Dragon.'" She continued moving through the center, panning in and around educational setups on the soil and trees making up the region.

"The most common story goes that the Jersey Devil was born to a woman named Mrs. Leeds in the 1730s somewhere in the eastern part of the Barrens. She'd already had twelve kids and didn't want any more, so she cursed this one. And it was born a hideous creature that flew away into the night. While the story is ridiculous, that hasn't stopped dozens of people from claiming to have seen the monster over the years."

Turning off the camera, Mia continued leisurely through the exhibit before leaving and getting back in her car.

The next time Mia turned on the camera again, she was driving away from Batsto and the nature center. She once again continued her narration to the device in her passenger seat. "Even in modern times, people claim to see the Jersey Devil, or at least its leftovers. In the twenties, a taxi driver reported seeing a winged creature when he was fixing a flat tire. In 1980, a bunch of pigs were found dead right here in Wharton State Forest. Since there were no tracks or traces left behind, people blamed the creature. I want to learn why folklore, especially around this Devil, is so prevalent in this part of the state, and how it ties into the overall culture of the people of the Pine Barrens."

The pick-up turned into a clearing. The sun was setting, and the sky showed shades of pink and orange. A dirt road lined one side and thick forest the other. Mia walked around, searching for the best area to pitch her tent, still talking to her invisible audience.

"The soil here is sandy and acidic, making traditional farming difficult. The colonists who first settled here were usually considered the lowest levels of society, including people who made moonshine or who'd deserted from the army. Most lived off the land, and many still do, hunting, fishing, and harvesting fruit like cranberries. Blueberries are one of the most common crops produced in the state," she said, pointing to the bright green bushes speckled with the fruit.

Mia turned off the camera and focused on setting up her campsite. She pitched a small tent not too far from the pick-up truck, laying tarps underneath and overtop. She had a portable campfire in the truck bed, which she removed and set up.

As the flames grew, Mia added one more comment to her video. "This is my campsite for the next two nights. It's a good location because I'm pretty deep into the forest, certainly farther in than most people go. I haven't seen any other campers around here either, so I shouldn't have to worry about being disturbed. Tomorrow, I'm going to conduct some interviews with local people. But for now, I'm exhausted."

After eating a can of beans and a sandwich she had packed earlier, she put out the fire and went into her tent, falling fast asleep.

Some hours later, in the middle of the night, Mia was awoken. Reaching around in the dark tent, she grabbed her camera, turning on its night vision to record and allow her to see better. She pointed it at her face, which glowed eerily green on screen.

She whispered, addressing the camera, "I was just woken up by a horrible scream. It sounded like someone or something in incredible pain. In 1960, residents of May's Landing reported similar noises and attributed them to the Jersey Devil. But we know now that they, and probably the ones I just heard, are actually the sounds of foxes mating. Not particularly scary, but definitely startling to wake up to."

Shaking her head with a slight smile, Mia turned off the camera and settled back down to sleep.

The next morning, the world was bright again. Mia left her campsite early to hike down one of the local trails. To her left, a stream quietly meandered by. Sunlight shone down, reflecting off the ochre-colored water. She heard birds singing from all directions, and the small plants around the edge of the streambed danced subtly in the wind as insects hopped from one to another.

Once again, she picked up her camera and began narrating the world around her. "See how the water looks reddish? That's from high iron levels. Some people call it 'cedar water.' This area is basically a massive swamp. The sandy soil produces near-pristine groundwater but makes it difficult to grow crops, which explains why the Pines was never developed into agricultural land like the rest of south Jersey."

As she made her way down the forest path, the thumping of her backpack against her shoulders became rhythmic. The burnt stumps of cedar, oak, and pine trees came into view.

"Forest fires are really common here and a natural part of the ecosystem," Mia said to the camera. "There are tons of animals down here too, bald eagles, tree frogs, even river dFdotters."

Mia walked silently as the path became less obvious and more overgrown. The camera picked up sounds of her breathing and the continued noises of nature's inhabitants as she traversed deeper into the forest.

Suddenly, Mia stopped moving and swung the camera around to the right. Slightly off the path, she pointed and zoomed in on a moist soil patch. Half a dozen prints were visible in dirt.

"Look at these!" Mia said to herself, panning the camera over each one. "See how they look hoof-like on the bottom, but then they sort of split at the top? I don't know what kind of creature would make a print like this." She investigated the area around the prints, finding no other tracks coming or going amongst the shrubbery.

"In 1909, there was this crazed panic because a bunch of people were finding signs of the Devil, many of them hooved footprints that maybe even looked something like these. It was all over the state from Bordentown to Mount Holly, Burlington, Gloucester, and Woodbury. The press had a field day, especially since some of the tracks were found on roofs and other difficult-to-reach areas, but then disappeared, leading to the belief that the creature could also fly. I don't know what made these tracks, but it would certainly be freaky to find them on my roof, especially if I only had a turn-of-the-century education."

Mia continued hiking for another hour, hoping the path would lead her to a half-hidden home where she could interview locals. Instead, she only saw more trees.

Suddenly, a loud noise came from just above her, like the sound of giant wings flapping, followed by a dark shadow. Mia let out a little shriek and took off. Her foot got caught on a rock, and she fell onto her left side.

Carefully getting up, Mia brushed the dirt off her scratched palms. She sat down on the path and clicked the camera on, setting it down next to her, propped slightly upward.

She pulled her left knee up to examine it, wiping away the blood flowing down her shin with a navy bandana from her backpack.

"So, this is embarrassing," she said to the camera, "but I spooked myself back there. I heard something in the woods, and then there was this shadow as it flew by. It looked huge, but I'm sure it was just a turkey vulture or something. Anyway, I freaked and tripped over a rock," Mia said sheepishly.

She reached behind her and grabbed a green plant. "This is sphagnum moss. Soldiers used it in the American Revolution for bandages. Since my first aid kit is back at the tent, I'm going to see if I can use it to stop some of the bleeding."

Mia rinsed the earthy material with water from her canteen and laid it carefully on her wound. She winced while tying the bandana around the moss to hold it in place. Hobbling, Mia stood upright and clicked off the camera, putting it away inside her bag. Turning around to head back to camp, Mia began walking.

For three hours, she had been following what she thought was the same trail, but somehow on her hike back, nothing seemed familiar. Eventually, she realized that she should have arrived back at her campsite some time ago. She must have made a wrong turn somewhere. The monoculture of the forest was confusing, and she breathed deeply, trying to stay calm.

A twig snapped behind her, and she whipped her head around. Far off in the forest, there were two glowing red orbs shining through the underbrush. Mia blinked twice, hoping to clear her vision, but the certainty of what she was seeing only cemented itself in her mind. She took off running.

Half a mile later, Mia stopped. She looked around, thankfully not seeing anything alarming.

"Okay, there is definitely something weird going on out here," her voice was somewhere above a whisper, and she gasped for breath between words.

Mia took out her camera once again, finding comfort in her routine. She turned it on and shakily faced forward. "It's already 6 p.m., and I'm still miles from my campsite. I can't even say which direction, to be honest, since I got super turned around. I don't know what I just saw, but it was something big with glowing eyes. A black bear, maybe? I don't know, but I didn't stick around to find out."

The trees seemed unusually dark and sinister against the backdrop of the setting sun. Mia was walking as fast as she could while hobbling from her injury. Her head turned back and forth as she inspected the tree line on either side of the path.

As her arm lowered to her side, the camera pointed behind Mia, capturing the path behind her. It was not a well-maintained trail, barely visible amongst overgrown weeds and rocks. Each time she bounced her injured leg, the camera would rise to catch the darkening view behind Mia. *Thump. Thump. Thump.*

Suddenly—unbeknownst to Mia—the trail behind her was no longer empty. A dark shape blocked out what little sunlight was left, creating a looming shadow on the camera. The skin on the back of Mia's neck prickled, and she took in a breath, slowly turning. Her eyes widened as she noticed the dark presence.

She stepped back carefully, but the sound of breaking glass made her wince. Glancing down, Mia realized her foot had landed on an old glass jug, likely used to hold moonshine, as was common in the Pines. Her head snapped up again. Two pricks of red had appeared in the shadow, giving it a clear animalistic form. With horror, Mia realized they were the same pair of eyes she'd seen before.

She took off running, willing herself not to look back as a high-pitched, blood-curdling scream followed her. The sky continued to darken as Mia ran faster than her injured leg should have allowed her to. She only stopped when she spotted an old fire tower in a clearing up ahead. Pausing at the base of the tower's ladder, Mia looked around. When she didn't see any creature, she decided to climb up.

The rungs were wooden, and she was terrified they would give way under her weight, but thankfully they held. Mia hoped she could get to the top and hide out up there. When she reached the shelter at the top, she pushed and banged at the wooden door. It wouldn't budge.

"Damn it," Mia cursed to herself. The inside of the tower was either locked or rotted shut. She craned her neck around, hoping to see over the trees and at least figure out what direction she should go.

In the distance past a creek, but not too far off, Mia noticed what looked like a cabin. She prayed it was an occupied house rather than something abandoned. Quickly, she mentally calculated her next move. Mia would climb down the ladder and make her way through the small meadow, swim across the water, and then go through the patch of woods to get to the structure.

Taking a deep breath, Mia started making her way down the ladder. With only the last lingering bit of sunlight in the air, she carefully stepped one foot down after another, hoping to stay quiet and not stumble. She hit solid ground and turned in the direction of the cabin.

Hunching over in a desperate attempt to make

herself appear less obvious in the meadow, Mia began quickly shuffling toward the creek. A dark shadow covered the moon's glow. Eventually, her eyes determined its shape, and she noticed in horror the large wings.

Mia took off at a full sprint as the sound of flapping wings grew closer and the shadow grew larger. It felt like minutes for her to reach the creek bed, but it was really no more than ten seconds. Scanning the bank, Mia spotted an overturned wooden canoe. Quickly, she raced toward it and pulled it behind her as she backed up into the creek. The coolness of the water soaked into her feet and legs, and she kept moving deeper.

Holding her breath, she slipped under the water's surface and came up underneath the canoe. There was enough space for her to float with her nose and mouth above the surface. Standing in the dark water under a dome of wood was terrifying, but Mia couldn't imagine it being worse than what was facing her outside.

Slowly, she shuffled her feet across the bottom of the creek, praying it wouldn't get deeper. She tried to ignore the feeling of slime and stone against her legs and stay as quiet as possible, moving painstakingly sluggishly as to not draw attention to herself.

Eventually, the water level receded, and Mia knew she had reached the other side. She once again slipped underwater and swam beyond the canoe. Peeking up over the surface, she didn't spot the creature anywhere. Quickly, Mia climbed out of the creek and took off running through the patch of forest that separated her and the cabin.

Her injured leg ached, and her lungs cried for her to stop, but Mia kept moving. Finally, she reached the structure she had seen from the fire tower. It was an old-fashioned log cabin. There were no lights on inside.

She slowed as she approached the structure, looking for any signs that someone might be in there and able to help her. Hanging around the perimeter of the decrepit building were paper lanterns. Mia approached one and looked closely at it, noticing crude drawings of a dark, winged shape that looked suspiciously like her pursuer.

She rushed to the front door and banged, only to notice that it was nailed shut. Glancing at the windows told her they too were closed off. Whether there was someone in there or not, they did not want Mia, or anyone else, to join them.

She darted off the porch, intending to look for another way into the cabin, or at least another hiding place, when an inhuman scream pierced the air. Mia covered her ears with her hands to mute what sounded like metal scraping against metal.

With a *whoosh*, the creature landed twenty feet away. Mia's eyes widened. She saw now how incredibly huge and unnatural it looked. Leathery wings spread at least ten feet in either direction from the solid, hairy body. Those piercing red eyes were back, directed right at her down a long muzzle. The creature opened its mouth, exposing odd-shaped teeth, and sniffed the air.

Mia grasped for her camera, hoping to at least capture some evidence of what was going on. Too late, she realized that it was completely soaked through from her foray across the creek and wouldn't turn on. Tossing the useless device aside, Mia looked around, spotting a large stick. She picked it up, brandishing it like a baseball bat. She was out of options, and this was her last stand.

The Devil screamed again, lifting off the ground, launching itself toward Mia. She swung the branch, and everything went black.

Salt

The spirits follow me closely. The only thing that keeps them away, keeps me safe, is salt. I wear a pouch around my waist filled with the rocky white substance. Anytime I hear or feel a presence behind me, I grab a handful and throw it over my shoulder. If a spirit is there, it sizzles and burns under the sodium chloride.

I am alone in the house; its occupants fled days ago. They called me here to cleanse their home and rid it of the spirits. What most people don't know is that ghosts are everywhere. We can never escape the souls of those who have departed. But not all of them must be kept away. Some of them are evil, like the ones that drove the family out. These are the ones I call spirits. These are the ones I am here to exorcise.

The day is hot and humid. The world waits on a precipice of a storm, the air crackling with intensity. Sirens blare in the distance. The air has been stirring, and the rain is slowly starting to come down. It is midday and should be bright with sunlight, but the sky is only gray.

As the wind picks up, it blows the white curtain hanging over the window back and forth, turning it from a ship's sail into a tight skin and back again. I watch it breathe in and out like a pair of lungs. Suddenly, when the air sucks the curtain back toward the window, it does not lay flat. Instead, it molds into a humanoid shape, betraying the presence of a spirit.

I turn quickly, averting my eyes from what lay underneath. You cannot look at them, because once your eyes lock, they have you in their grasp. Instead, you must fight them as invisible beings. I often imagine what they must look like. Are they translucent nonhuman beings? Specters of long-dead witches? Are they invisible altogether? I will never know and cannot know unless I want to die.

My mother was a shaman. She taught me how to find the evil spirits and how to get rid of them. This practice comes with a price, though: all who set out to defeat evil end up attracting it. That is why I wear the salt.

I reach into my pouch, feeling the comfort of the grains between my fingers before flinging them behind me. A slight hiss retorts, telling me the spirit has been chastised. I begin to say the ancient prayers passed down to me from my mother and hers before. I continue flinging salt as the words flow from my mouth, weakening the evil presence.

I remember the warm touch of my mother's hand on mine as she guided me through the motions, teaching me how to be stronger than the spirits. I remember the calm in her voice when she faced down evil. I had resolved to be like her, and my soul aches in her absence.

Behind me, I feel the physical presence of another soul. The hairs on the back of my neck stand as it gets closer. I fight the urge to turn, to look death in the face. My mother is gone, so now I must fight alone.

A tear slips down my cheek. I do not wipe it away; its salinity will protect me. I continue praying and throw more salt.

Green Forest, White Snow

Once upon a time, there lived two sisters in a land of dense forests and cold winters. Their names were Alyy and Belizna, and although they were close in age and sentiment, the two girls were very different. Alyy preferred summers, when meadows were full of wildflowers and bees hummed in her ear. Belizna loved nothing more than curling up next to the fire on a cold, snowy day to read her favorite tales. Their mother was a poor widow who loved both of her daughters unconditionally.

The woman was a healer, ostracized by the pious and superstitious villagers who mistook her lack of a husband and skills with herbs for sin. Their cottage was on the edge of the forest, some lengths away from the rest of the village. Despite this outward resentment, their front door was often imposed upon by villagers looking for cures to any number of ailments. The woman taught her daughters about living things, and life taught them about discrimination.

One winter was exceptionally cold, and everyone suffered for it. Villagers burned through their woodpiles faster than ever before, and food was carefully rationed. These were sturdy folk who were used to living in frigid temperatures, but even they were unprepared for what befell them that year.

You see, the children were dying. One by one across the village, children took sick to their beds. No matter how much wood their parents burned or how many quilts were piled atop them, they could not get warm.

The worst part came after a week of steadily declining health. When all hope seemed lost, and it seemed the parents would not be able to save the children, their families were dealt an even bigger blow. Their prodigy simply vanished.

Mothers tore at their hair, and fathers cursed the heavens. Their children disappeared, and they were left with no bodies to bury, merely cold, empty beds.

After a few months, every household had been struck with this malady but one: the widow's cottage remained untouched. Alyy and Belizna had color in their cheeks and warmth in their bones. Upon realizing this, the villagers turned their anger toward the healing woman.

"Witch!" they called her. Because her children were the only ones to avoid the village's terrible fate, they surmised she must be the cause behind it. No medicine or natural cures could bring their children back, and the disappearing bodies meant only one thing: dark magic.

One especially cold night, there was a banging on the door. The villagers had gathered outside the widow's humble abode, their torches reflecting in the glass windowpanes. They forced their way inside and grabbed the woman. She tried to calm her crying daughters as the crowd dragged her away to be jailed.

Left alone in the quiet darkness as the crowd's noise receded, the two sisters stared at each other with wide eyes, their bodies shaking.

"We have to go after them and get her back!" Alyy said, her eyes fiery.

"But we cannot fight the entire village!" her sister replied in a strained voice.

"We must do something!"

Belizna thought for a moment, hands clutching the hair at her scalp, before responding. "We must prove to them that Mother did not harm their children. We need to find out what happened to them."

They decided to set off into the forest, for surely the answers they sought could only be found there. Belizna packed a bag full of brown bread, hard cheese, and vegetables they had preserved from the garden. Alyy sharpened their ax and hung it through her belt, along with a few coins they had stashed away.

Together, they made their way through the dense conglomeration of spruces and firs. Their small feet left identical tracks in the snow. Branches caught on their capes and let loose powdery flakes as they walked by.

Traveling through the rich forest, the sisters came upon many animals, to whom they would kindly inquire about the missing children.

"Excuse me, Mr. Squirrel, but do you know where the sick children from the village have gone?"

"Hello, Ms. Fox. We're looking for the missing children. Do you know where they may be?"

They asked chipmunks, lemmings, deer, and elk. None had any answer for them. After many hours of walking, night fell. As the sun disappeared from the sky, they were faced on every side by dark walls of coniferous trees. The girls decided to hunker down for the night in an abandoned den, falling fast asleep from exhaustion.

As morning dawned, the sisters suddenly awoke to a dark shadow and a deep roar. They rose in shock at the sight of a massive brown bear.

"What are you doing in my den?" the bear asked them.

"We are terribly sorry to disturb you, Mr. Bear," Belizna said quickly.

Her sister continued, "We simply needed shelter for the night and did not know this was occupied."

The bear looked between the two sisters, one cloaked in red and the other in white. With a huff, he settled down next to them. "You may stay here, but I'm afraid I have no food to share. I have been starving for some days now."

Alyy and Belizna looked at each other and nodded. Belizna began opening the bag while Alyy responded, "You may partake in some of our provisions, although we don't have much."

The three of them quietly held their repast, enjoying the sounds of the forest awakening around them.

"Why are you so deep in this wood?" the bear finally asked them.

The sisters explained their quest to find the missing children and clear their mother's name.

The bear made to leave the den, gesturing to the sisters to follow him. They packed up their satchels quickly, and all three emerged into the sunlight.

Silently, the bear lumbered north, and the two girls trailed behind him. After about an hour of treading deeper into the forest, they came upon a secluded cave. The bear entered but motioned for the girls to stay behind. Waiting, they looked around, noting the lack of animals this deep into the woods. It was cold, and their breath swirled from their lips in white mist.

A few minutes later, the bear reemerged from the cavern. In his paw was a long icicle. It glittered in the sun's rays that managed to peek through the dense coniferous canopy. It was sharp enough to wound even the toughest hide.

Gingerly, the bear handed the icicle to Alyy, saying, "The White Witch has stolen the children of your village. She is very powerful and can only be defeated with a weapon of her own making. You must plunge this deep into her chest, where her missing heart used to sit, to slay her and release your comrades."

Alyy clutched the weapon and nodded gravely. Belizna had fear in her eyes but set her jaw with determination. The sisters thanked the bear and began walking north in the direction he pointed them, toward the White Witch.

They walked for hours, their feet aching and cheeks

rubbed raw by the wind. Snowflakes flew at all angles through the air like honeybees. They rained down on the girls, so cold the sharp edges of ice left tiny cuts on their pale skin. Still, the sisters moved forward.

Eventually, the forest thinned, and the deep emerald faded away into white as they approached a barren patch of snow-covered land studded with sharp, icy rocks.

Quietly, the two tiptoed to a large boulder, peeking around the side to the clearing. There they saw the White Witch. She wore a thick white coat made of pristine fur and sat in a cream-colored sleigh lined in silver and gold. Two glistening pearl-colored horses were harnessed to the sleigh. The witch's skin was the most translucent of whites, paler even than milk from sick cows. Behind her stood a ghost horde of children, souls of the dead wavering in the cold wind. The children of their village had become a slave army to this evil being. Their eyes were shallow, leeched of both warmth and soul.

Knowing they had only one chance to defeat the White Witch and save the children—and their mother—from their horrendous fates, the sisters looked at each other and nodded.

Belizna stepped out from behind the rock. As if the warmth from her body alerted the witch to her presence, the villain turned toward her.

"Let the children go," Belizna said in a voice not as loud as she'd hoped it would be.

The White Witch cocked her head slightly, intrigued

by the small annoyance. When she smiled, it was cold, and she bared shards of diamonds as teeth.

Belizna's heart nearly beat out of her chest as the witch floated effortlessly toward her. She willed her shaky knees to be steady and took in a gulp of air. The witch reached out a hand, her long white fingers ending in sharpened silver nails. Slowly, she ran one of them along Belizna's cheek, smiling her sharp fangs again.

Suddenly, Alyy jumped out from behind the boulder. Her red cape blurred through the air as her body made contact with the witch. Both fell to the ground in a heap, and an inhuman scream pierced the air. Alyy stood quickly, backing up and taking her sister's hand.

The icicle was sticking out of the White Witch's chest. Instead of blood, out from the wound seeped a liquid silver. Her eyes widened in pain, and her mouth twisted with her scream. Wide-eyed, the girls watched as the witch's pale skin lost any semblance of color. Her entire being turned crystal clear before shattering into a million pieces.

After, it was quiet. The girls smiled at each other and turned back to the children. Gleefully, they watched as their peers came back to life in front of their eyes, their bodies gaining form, their cheeks color, and their eyes happiness. Laughing together, the children of the village set off together back home.

Their arrival sparked the single most joyful moment in the village's history. Parents wept with relief, and children clung to them, happy to feel the cold that reminded them of how alive they were. Belizna and Alyy went immediately to their mother, who was tied up in the village square. They broke her bindings and embraced in a tight hug, thankful that no one had been injured.

From that day forward, the village people looked on the widow and her courageous daughters with respect. They no longer slunk in shame to their door for remedies but instead paid handsomely for the healer's wares. Every winter, the two sisters made their way deep into the forest to bring food to the helpful bear. The village remained in peace for many years, and they all lived happily ever after.

Conversations in the
Back of an Uber

She could feel all the pillars that held their relationship together, which had once been as firm as cement, crumble beneath her as if they were nothing more than cotton candy in her mouth. She struggled to speak, working her tongue around the crystallized pink sugar that had already quickly disappeared along with her reassurances, leaving a grainy feeling.

"This was your idea."

"I know. But it was a bad idea."

Staring out the window, she watched the lights of Manhattan blur together, mixing with the raindrops that slowly began appearing on the glass. She traced one's journey down the glass with her index finger; the red polish there turned an angry merlot color in the darkness of the vehicle.

"I don't want to lose you."

She didn't respond.

"I'm sorry I ever suggested this."

"Me too."

She faced forward, looking at the driver's phone on the dashboard, watching the time slowly tick downward until they reached their destination. She knew, somehow—felt deep in her bones—that their arrival at the apartment coincided with the ending of their relationship.

"What do we do now?"

"I don't know."

Her brain was racing, but her mood was oddly calm. A sense of clarity had settled inside her, covering her with a liquid layer, like she was floating under water.

Her girlfriend reached for her hand. She pulled it away, crunching her hand into a fist at her side, sealing it up like she should have done her heart months ago.

"Please talk to me."

"I don't know what else there is to say."

"Say you love me."

A beat passed. "I love you."

"Please don't leave me."

No response.

The vehicle pulled to a stop. The driver didn't say anything; he merely accepted the next alert from his app. The silence inside the car was broken only by the pitter-pattering of raindrops and the hum of the car's engine.

Her breathing was loud and dangerous. She felt her girlfriend's eyes boring into her but wouldn't turn to look at her. Neither wanted to move, knowing that as soon as one stepped out into the wet night, it signified the ending of their journey together.

Taking a deep breath, she put her hand to the door. Exhaling, she pushed it open and welcomed the cold.

She Has Her Cake
and Eats It Too

uck you, cake, she thought to herself. Carrie was practically drooling over the store-bought, pink-frosted chocolate concoction. It was most likely from a chain supermarket and lacked a small bakery's refined taste. Still, it looked like the best thing in the world to her. Another random coworker's birthday meant another celebration with a mediocre baked good. Chocolate this time, because it was Andy's favorite.

Carrie used to not mind these little moments that broke up the workday's monotony and provided sugar highs for the afternoons. Now these moments were torture, like holding a carrot in front of the horse, except the carrot was carbs and sugar, and the horse was a chubby twenty-eight-year-old woman who worked in accounting.

Carrie wondered how those little ganache swirls would melt on her tongue. She guessed that the rose-colored icing would stick to her lips, and she would have to lick it off. Her stomach grumbled as she thought of her own lunch compared to the beautiful, moist, sugary dessert tempting her from the conference room. Her meager salad with fat-free dressing and sliced apples sprinkled with cinnamon were not nearly appetizing enough to make her look the other way.

For the past five or so months, she'd been gaining weight and didn't know why. Her pants fit tighter and tighter, and her stomach bulged a bit more in front and on the sides every month. She knew she wasn't entirely unattractive with her bright blue eyes and thick chestnut curls, but her body was simply not cooperating.

She'd gone to the doctor, of course. They'd taken her measurements and warned her about the dangers of being overweight. She'd scoffed at this at first, knowing she was not "overweight." Not really. She thought of herself more as "chubby." Still, it was not acceptable, and this fat had to go. Carrie had cut out nearly all of her favorite foods, including chocolate cake and anything else deemed unhealthy, and she had upped her workouts to four times a week. But nothing she was doing was working. In fact, Carrie was still *gaining* weight.

Carrie looked around the office at the bodies that filled it. Andy, the skinny birthday boy, was always pleasant, if a bit too perky in the morning hours. Maria was the queen bee of the office social scene, and no one ever pissed her off since she was in charge of organizing these little birthday celebrations. She dressed impeccably enough to hide the extra ten or fifteen pounds that gathered on her hips and thighs. Todd, the accountant, was nice enough but only seemed to talk about sports. He looked like the typical gym bro who maybe had one too many beers on the weekends: fit and muscular but with the slight bulge of his belly.

Then there was Zaralena.

Carrie hated her. Zaralena was gorgeous. She was tall and thin, but not too thin—she had a killer body with just the right balance of slender muscle and feminine curve to fit in on the Victoria's Secret runway. Carrie quietly snorted as she further inspected her co-worker, noticing how the other woman's new summer wardrobe showed off her svelte curves. Zaralena helped herself to some cake, the sleeve of her fuchsia blazer nearly grazing the granulated frosting as she sliced a piece. Carrie's eyes narrowed into slits.

Four months before, the entire office had undertaken a weight loss challenge, and despite all her dieting, Carrie had only managed to look bigger and more bloated. Meanwhile, perfect Zaralena seemed to eat whatever she wanted while the weight melted off. Every day she indulged in take-out, fast food, or pizza, and still, she had transformed into a supermodel. It was incredibly baffling to Carrie, who should have been the one losing weight since she was the one putting in the effort.

Carrie made her way to the women's bathroom and, upon finding it empty, stepped onto the communal scale (a cruel addition, if you asked her). Looking down, she fought back the urge to throw it out the window. There was no way she had gained three pounds in a week. With all her dieting and cardio workouts, it wasn't possible. It wasn't like she could use the "muscle weighs more than fat" excuse either; her jeans were just as tight on her bulging midsection. The rage bubbled up inside her at the unfairness of it all.

Leaving the bathroom, Carrie walked away from the breakroom where most of her coworkers remained, and instead turned toward the collection of cubicles making up their office's main floor. Pausing at one boxed compartment, Carrie looked around and, seeing no one watching her, quickly sat down at her coworker's desk.

Hidden behind the flimsy gray walls, Carrie looked around at the space. Zaralena's cubicle was disgustingly cliché: a motivational quote calendar, a mousepad covered in kittens, and a small pink bag presumably filled with makeup products. Carrie snorted to herself as she moved the mouse, activating the screen. *Damn*, she thought to herself as she noted the dozens of open tabs in the browser.

She began exploring the windows, noticing much of it was typical work-related content. After a few clicks, Carrie came across Facebook. Zaralena was logged into her personal account, and the screen showed a private group called the "Hellsnick Coven." Her eyebrows shot up. Carrie checked behind her, but no one was approaching, so she continued scrolling through the page. Seeing nothing particularly magical or forbidden, she clicked to another tab.

The website looked like it had been designed ten years previously, its purple font curling around inserted images and links. The language was not English—nor anything else Carrie could identify—but the drawings on the page were clear enough. They looked to be sketches scanned from an old book. The first was the silhouette of two women; the next was a basket of fruit, bread, and a bunch of items she couldn't recognize.

The third image was the two women again, but this time, the one on the right was significantly wider in girth than the one on the left. *Is this some sort of dieting spell?* Carrie thought to herself. *Maybe this is how Zaralena manages to lose all that weight while eating whatever she wants.*

Carrie's eyes turned to the carnation-colored bag to her right. Unzipping the sequined pouch, Carrie pulled out a root of some kind, smelling and then dropping it back in. Next came a bag of unidentifiable herbs. *Maybe she really is a witch*, Carrie thought.

Continuing her search through the bag, Carrie pulled out what looked like a sketch of two women. It resembled the one she had seen on the website but was hand-drawn and more detailed. On a scrap of paper was a thin woman with short dark hair and a shorter, plumper figure next to her. Carrie stared harder at the second silhouette, noticing swirly lines extending from her head.

She reached up to touch her own curls, wild and loose, as she usually wore them. She was shorter than Zaralena. Carrie's heart rate sped as the wheels turned in her head. Zaralena had used some kind of evil magic to make Carrie gain weight while she kept it off. There was no other possible explanation. Her eyesight blazed red.

Getting up from the desk, Carrie haphazardly dropped the piece of paper. She walked swiftly but silently into the kitchen, her mind flashing back to all the delicious meals she'd had to watch Zaralena consume over the past few weeks while her waistline just kept shrinking. She thought about her own steadily increasing body fat percentage, about the hours spent on the treadmill, about that pink frosted chocolate cake she'd denied herself.

The people left in the kitchen looked up as Carrie entered, and the conversation stopped at the odd look on her face. Zaralena was leaning against the table, licking pink icing off her perfectly manicured fingers.

Carrie couldn't speak. She reached down and pulled the knife out of its chocolatey home and, in one quick beat, plunged it into Zaralena's chest. Zaralena's eyes widened as a red stain bloomed from the blade's entry point. She fell to the floor as the rest of her coworkers stood motionless in shock.

Looking calmly down at Zaralena's immobile form, Carrie bent to remove the knife, which made a slushing noise as it ejected from the other woman's body. The blade still had dark chocolate crumbs and smooth pink icing stuck to it among the scarlet blood.

Carrie licked it, savoring the taste of copper and sugar.

Sweet, grainy, wonderful sugar.

Bride in Shadows

Wind whipped through the gray sky, taking with it the now withered bouquet. The bundle of flowers hopped along as though in tune with some silent song that only the dead could hear. The nosegay had traveled far from its prospective owner, but she no longer cared or noticed its absence. The bride walked alone in the gray.

Her silhouette, shrouded in lace, could only look forward as she walked. She did not stop to ponder outside of her vision as the periphery was of no matter to her anymore. She had left all reason at the altar with her shattered hopes. The future she had once seen so clearly was now a wisp of smoke as its timeline fell away like a burnt match.

Leafless trees lined her path, their branches thin and spread like capillaries against the gray sky speckled with pale clouds floating by. Small sticks curled slightly into her hair like the withered fingers of a long-dead corpse. The once-bride resented the sun for shining, its rays serving as reminders of happiness that had evaded her and slipped through her fingers like sand.

Deep in the woods, the earth opened up in welcome to her, creating a hole with walls and descending stairs of dirt and darkness, and she made her way into the cool damp of the underworld. The walls became stones with dark, viscous material bleeding through their cracks and silhouettes of faces appearing and disappearing with the slightest turn of one's head.

She continued in her aimless march, a gossamer veil trailing behind, iridescent in the fading light. She walked forward and down, down, down into the very depths of Hell itself. For she was a bride still and would be united. If she couldn't have the one who had her heart, why not parlay with the Devil herself?

After many hours that may have been days, the rejected bride came upon a throne of bones. The reigning sovereign herself greeted her in her despair.

"Bear witness to my sins and devour me of my desires."

The bride offered up thin, translucently pale wrists with blue veins to the horned god of the underworld.

"Drain me of my life-blood; I have no heart to replenish it."

The sleek queen rose, her feminine form both dangerous and sensual in its power, her black lips curling back into a snarl, revealing sharp points of ivory underneath. Floating toward the bride, she brought the scents of chrysanthemum and burning embers with her. A flash, and her mouth was upon the bride's wrist flesh, delicately brushing against the once-pristine sleeve of her gown.

Drops of blood formed instantly and dripped to the floor, solidifying in their journey downward and becoming pebbles of rubies as they bounced away into the shadows. The woman's eyes lit with fire for the first time since she had been abandoned at the sanctum. She was a bride no longer, her soul now one with the darkness she had embraced.

Cat Scratch Fever

I

"God, you're such a lesbian," moaned Missy in mock frustration. She was standing with her arms crossed, rolling her eyes at her girlfriend.

Angie gave a sheepish grin and placed the hot pink ceramic "Cat Mom" mug back on the shelf. She moved on to shop the rows of vintage jewelry and other assembled knickknacks. The next shelf contained a porcelain feline figure painted in orange stripes. Angie's eyes welled with tears as she stroked its head.

"It looks just like Seamus," she said quietly. Wiping the water from her eyes, she retracted her hand. "Sorry, I'm just being a baby."

Missy squeezed her partner's shoulder and responded, "Oh, babe, it's okay. I know you miss him; he was your baby for so long."

About a week before, Angie had started dropping hints about getting a new cat. Or cats. Missy wasn't really on board. She had nothing against cats per se, but she hated the litter box upkeep and annoying 4 a.m. wake-up calls. However, she knew her partner would go to the shelter and bring home the first sad set of whiskers she spotted. As a compromise, Missy had agreed to go with Angie to the new cat café that had opened up in their favorite small town, New Faith.

The two women stepped out of the shop and made their way down the street. The entire town was decorated with orange pumpkins and homemade scarecrows in anticipation of the upcoming holiday. Red and yellow leaves blew across the street, giving the feeling of being in a picturesque Hallmark movie.

Angie pulled her rainbow scarf tighter and zipped up the faux leather jacket she was wearing over a vintage Ghostbusters tee. Her lavender hair flew about in the autumn wind, getting itself caught in the many cartilage rings that adorned her ears.

As they made their way across the busy street, narrowly avoiding a group of bikers who clearly didn't respect the rules of a crosswalk, Missy spotted the cat café, Kitty Kitty.

"There it is! Next to the witch shop," she said, pointing out the town's newest establishment.

Angie swatted the taller woman on the arm. "Don't call it that! It's a Wiccan store."

"Okay, well whatever it's called, I can smell the patchouli from here."

Angie laughed as they made their way up to and through the door of Kitty Kitty. The space was smaller than she'd expected, with walls painted pale yellow and floors covered in cat trees, cat beds, and cat toys galore.

"Hi! I have a reservation for two for Angela Garcia," Angie said, looking around. There were a few others already in the establishment, including a young couple trying to coax a sleeping calico awake with a feather toy, to no avail.

"You just need to sign these waivers," replied the thin man at the counter. He handed over two clipboards and went through the rules in a bored voice. He mentioned that coffee and tea were available, gesturing to the "café" that was really just a Keurig and a tin of cookies.

Missy shook her head, since she had filled up on vegan scones while Angie had tried to convince the owner of Twig & Leaf to hire her for their baking needs. Angie and her sister co-owned a vegan catering service, but baking was Angie's main passion. Luckily, Missy had a strong enough sweet tooth to take on all the test treats and sugary mistakes.

Missy and Angie slowly walked through the café, noticing the framed photos on the wall featuring each cat available for adoption, along with their background stories. The wall to the left was covered in items for sale, including cat-meme postcards and feline pun T-shirts. They made their way to the back of the shop, where the cats were lounging in various stages of sleep. She noted a few chonky boys lying on the tallest cat tree in the corner and a younger-looking slim brown tabby that appeared to be half bored and half curious about the newcomers.

"Oh, hey there, little buddy. Who are you?"

Missy turned when she heard Angie cooing behind her. She was kneeling down, trying to lure a tuxedo cat out of its corner. Unlike most of the other adult felines in the room, this cat was awake and alert as it cocked its head at the sound of Angie's voice.

Missy walked over and crouched down next to her girlfriend.

"What's your name?" Missy asked before glancing back at the wall to find the cat's ID. She looked over each photo but was confused to find none that matched this black-and-white animal with the piercing green eyes. She shrugged, assuming the cat was too new to have had its profile posted yet.

Angie reached out slowly and pet the cat on the head. It responded by rubbing up against her hand. She gave it a behind-the-ears scratch, which elicited soft purring and more interest from the sleek animal.

"Aw, babe, look at this sweetheart," Angie said.

Missy tentatively reached out a hand to pet the animal. All of a sudden, the cat lurched forward, attaching itself to Missy's forearm and clamping its jaw down on the sensitive skin there.

"Ow, what the hell!" she shouted, falling back and shaking the animal off her. The cat scurried off under one of the hiding places built into the back wall.

"Oh my god, are you okay?" Angie immediately grabbed Missy's arm for inspection. There were two deep-looking cuts from the cat's canines, surrounded by lighter scratches made by its claws. They were oozing blood that threatened to drip onto Missy's expensive jeans.

Applying pressure to the wound with her hand, Angie urged Missy to her feet and pulled her toward the front desk. "Can we get some bandages over here?" she half-shouted to the bored man who had checked them in.

He produced a basic first aid kit, and Angie pulled some packages of anti-bacterial gel out, as well as gauze and tape. She did the best she could to wrap the wound and then looked up at Missy. "You good?"

"Yeah, I just want to get out of here, please."

"Come on, let's go."

Angie and Missy left the café and stepped onto the sidewalk, greeted by the chilly air and warm sunshine. Turning to walk down the street, they noticed a figure standing in the doorway to the store next door—the "witch store," as Missy had called it. The tall, gray-haired woman eyed the girls suspiciously, her gaze immediately finding the bandage on Missy's arm that had spots of red seeping through it.

"Were you bit?" she asked without taking her eyes off the wound.

"Um, yeah," Missy replied.

"Which cat?"

"I don't know," she answered, annoyed. "The cat didn't have a name on the wall." After a few seconds, she hurriedly continued, "But it's fine. I'm sure the cat isn't bad or anything. I don't want them to put it down for this or anything like that." She was rambling.

Angie nudged her forward. "Don't worry, babe. We signed a waiver, and I'm sure they won't hurt the cat. It happens. Come on, let's get you home." She lightly pulled her girlfriend away from the cat café and the creepy lady next door and led her back to their car in the parking lot.

"This town is so weird," Missy muttered.

II

The next morning, Missy Lyonne yawned as she dried her freshly washed face in the bathroom. She put on her glasses and looked down to inspect the damage to her arm. When they'd gotten home the day before, Angie had washed the wound with antiseptic and re-bandaged it. It had finally stopped bleeding but still looked angry and fresh. Missy sighed, replaced the bandage, and walked into the bedroom.

Missy worked as a graphic designer for an interior decorating company. She considered herself the most alternative person at her office and made a particular effort to hide her tattoo sleeve from nosy coworkers. She chose a brown tweed blazer to go over a pale pink button-up. She winced as the fabric moved across her beat-up forearm. *Damn that cat.*

Making her way into the kitchen, Missy could smell

fresh coffee and reheated apple muffins. She stuffed one in her mouth and poured some of the French roast into her to-go cup. Angie was sitting at the table in front of her red MacBook decorated with stickers.

Missy bent down to kiss the shorter woman on the forehead, noting the abundance of open tabs on her screen, each presumably showing different cupcake flavors. Angie was always trying to come up with the tastiest and most unique flavor combinations. Missy liked classic red velvet best, but she would happily try any of her partner's concoctions.

Grabbing her satchel off the front table, she shouted a final goodbye and left the house. There was a thirty-minute drive from their place to downtown, where she worked. She felt her sore limbs stretch as she climbed into her Subaru, starting the engine and scrolling through Sirius XM stations. After settling on nineties grunge, Missy focused on the drive. She noticed how especially clear the sky was today. No, not the sky, the actual air seemed clearer.

She pushed her glasses up on her head and then back down on her nose. It felt crazy, but it was like she could see better. She could see street signs blocks away and a plane in the sky that normally would have looked like a moving dot. Shaking her head, she brushed the odd thoughts away. Maybe the city's new air pollution initiatives were finally paying off. It was good to know her vote counted in some ways, at least.

Missy pulled into her building's private parking garage, left her car on the P3 level, and made her way to the elevators that would deliver her to the fifth floor. Despite housing an interior design company, her workplace was surprisingly bereft of color and pattern. Interior design fads tended to come and go, and Missy guessed it made more sense for them to keep the space simple instead of swapping out salmon spots for lavender stripes for metallic ombre every time a new style started trending.

Missy settled into her corner nook. She had more space than most of the employees stationed in the open floor plan, with multiple screens to accompany her design software. Sitting down, she felt pain radiating through her left side. Missy did not handle pain well, and this cat injury was turning out to be worse than she'd originally thought. She grumbled to herself, angry that she had even allowed herself to go into a random café and pet strange animals.

Missy spent most of the morning catching up on emails and signing off on some final designs for the upcoming winter catalog. It felt weird to be working on Christmas-themed decor when Halloween was only a week away, but that was how these things got done in time. Missy rubbed her eyes and stretched her hands over her head, deciding she would take a break for lunch.

Sometime after her lunch hour, which she spent gossiping with coworkers in the breakroom, a message popped up on Missy's chat. "I don't feel like cooking tonight. Sadie's Bistro?" She smiled to herself, secretly glad that Angie wanted to eat out because she also didn't feel like cooking.

Taking a break from absentmindedly rubbing her sore arm, Missy typed a response: "I'll call and make a reservation for six o'clock."

Angie quickly replied with a smiley-face emoji. She was a great cook, but sometimes cooking all day for work made it difficult for Angie to even consider doing it again that night for their own dinner. Missy didn't mind, though, and she always jumped at the chance to eat out, even if her bank account protested.

By the time Missy pulled into the parking lot of Sadie's Bistro that evening, the sky had become dark, and the autumn chill had returned to the air. She parked, locked up, and started walking toward the restaurant.

A woman and her golden retriever were passing by on the sidewalk. When the dog spotted Missy, it pulled back its lips, revealing a snarl as it lifted its haunches. He began barking at her in a way that stopped her in her tracks.

"Charlie, stop that!" the dog's owner chided, pulling harshly on the leash. "I'm so sorry," she continued. "I don't know what's got into him. He usually loves people."

Missy gave a tight smile to reassure the lady but quickly kept walking, hoping to avoid any further interactions with the mutt. She was normally much more of a dog person, but today she just wasn't feeling it.

Walking into the small restaurant, Missy spotted

Angie sitting at their favorite table by the window. She joined her, and the two women comfortably chatted about their respective days before ordering their food and two glasses of sauvignon blanc.

After a delicious appetizer of olive tapenade on crostini, the waiter brought out the ladies' entrees. Angie had gotten her usual, the vegan pasta primavera, while Missy had ordered something different.

Angie eyed the plate in front of her other half. "I thought you didn't like fish," Angie said, crinkling her nose at the smell. She watched Missy pick up her fork and inspect the salty protein on her plate.

"I don't usually, but I don't know, I guess I was craving it tonight," her girlfriend replied.

Angie forehead creased as she watched Missy eat the pescatarian meal with surgical precision.

Later that evening, the couple was cuddled on the couch, watching their favorite black and white film, *Cat People.* They had turned off all the lights to "set the spooky mood," as Angie put it.

Pressing pause on the remote, Angie untangled herself from the shared blanket and stood up, "Want some more tea?" she asked.

Missy shook her head. Angie was already bounding out of the room. She set the kettle on the stove and, despite being full from dinner, started rummaging in the freezer.

"Hey, babe," she called, peering around the wall into the darkened living room. She stopped abruptly. Besides the stark glow from the television, the only other light in the room came from two glowing orbs on the couch. Her heart jumped and then calmed when she recognized the orbs as her girlfriend's eyes staring back at her.

Immediately, her blood began pulsing once more. Human eyes shouldn't have been glowing that way. She quickly turned the lights on.

"Yeah?" Missy answered casually. Her eyes looked normal in the warm light of the lamp.

"Uh, nothing," Angie replied, distracted. "Were you just . . . licking your arm?" she asked, trying not to sound too accusatory.

"I just spilled some tea on it," Missy shot back in a cursory tone.

Angie paused a beat. "Okay." She turned around and went back into the kitchen.

III

A few days later, after unsuccessfully organizing her baking ingredients for the next batch of test cupcakes, Angie realized she was too anxious to get any real work done. Missy had been up all night, first pacing the bedroom, then the living room, then who-knew-where. Angie could usually sleep through anything, but she was too worried about the insomnia her girlfriend seemed to be suffering from of late.

That wasn't the only weird thing going on with Missy either. Angie had noticed that her girlfriend seemed more temperamental and standoffish than usual, oddly quiet rather than her normally talkative self and prone to skittishness. The day before, she had spent almost ten minutes staring out the window, watching the birds at the feeder with an intense glare, barely blinking and never turning away. These behavioral changes scared Angie more than the wound on Missy's arm ever had.

She quietly left the kitchen and went out into the living room, sitting down on the couch and opening her MacBook. After browsing through some news sites, she hesitated for a second, then moved her mouse and typed "cat bite" into her search bar.

One website said that three-quarters of cat bites introduced bacteria into the wound. This could cause infections that spread through the body, even as severe as septicemia. But Missy didn't seem to have blood poisoning, and there was no indication that she had an infection of any kind. Angie kept scrolling.

Remembering that the feline had also gotten its claws into Missy's forearm, she changed her search to "cat scratch." According to the internet, there was something called "cat scratch fever." Apparently, five hundred people a year in the United States were hospitalized with the disease, also caused by unwanted bacteria. The sickness included body aches, loss of appetite, fatigue, and chills.

But none of this explained Missy's undefinably odd

behavior. Frustrated, Angie slammed the laptop shut. She couldn't just sit at home and drive herself nuts scouring the internet and relying on WebMD to tell her what was going on. Angie knew she needed to talk to an expert, but were there experts on this type of thing? Her mind ran in circles, considering doctors, psychologists, priests, veterinarians. Nothing seemed right.

Suddenly she had an idea. It might have been nothing, but it was the best lead she had, and if she was honest with herself, she had to get out of the house before she drove herself crazy.

Angie grabbed her keys off the counter, left the house, and got in her car, once again making the drive to New Faith. She parked her car (a much easier task to do in the middle of a weekday rather than during peak weekend brunch time) and headed for Kitty Kitty.

The same bored-looking man was at the counter.

"Hi, do you remember me? I was here a few days ago, and one of the cats attacked my girlfriend."

His professional voice did not mask the lack of care in his eyes when he spoke. "Yeah. But you signed the waiver, so—"

She interrupted him with a wave. "I'm not going to sue you, don't worry. I just wanted to get some background on the cat that bit her."

"Which one was it?"

"I don't know its name. It was a tuxedo. Black and white."

"We don't have any of those at the moment."

"But you did when we were here. Could it have been adopted?"

"Nope. No adoptions in the last week."

"Okay, well, a black-and-white cat definitely bit her. I saw it."

"You can look around and check the wall, but we don't have any tuxes right now."

Narrowing her eyes, Angie did just that. She looked in every nook and cranny and scanned every wall for a flier that might identify the mystery feline, but to no avail. There wasn't even a single cat that resembled the one she remembered interacting with.

Suddenly a thought popped into her head. The place could have removed the cat to remove their liability. They could be lying to her, knowing full well that a black-and-white cat with green eyes had attacked a customer, but feigning innocence. She supposed she was going to get nothing out of the guy behind the counter, so, grabbing a business card so she could contact the owner later, Angie left the café and walked outside.

As she moved down the sidewalk, Angie's eyes locked on the Wiccan store. She remembered the odd interaction with the woman outside on the day Missy had been bitten. On a whim, she turned toward the entrance and walked through the door, a bell jangling as she did so.

Feeling like she just walked into the magic shop from *Buffy the Vampire Slayer*, Angie was disappointed that instead of finding Giles and the Scooby Gang sitting around, there appeared to be no one else in the establishment.

She walked slowly past the overcrowded shelves and hanging displays, noting bags of hand-labeled herbs like devil's claw and marshmallow root. Angie's eye caught the sparkles from a table covered in gems of various colors and shapes.

Finally, the woman came out of the back entrance through a curtain of iridescent beads that Angie remembered having had in her own closet during the hippie-revitalization fad in the nineties.

"Hello, my name is Solange. How can I help you?" the woman asked in a neutral voice. She looked like one of the aunts from *Practical Magic*: long hair, long skirt, long necklaces, and an even longer glare.

"I need help," Angie began. After receiving no initial response from the woman, she continued, "It's my girlfriend. Something . . . weird is happening to her."

"This is about the cat bite." Solange's reply was less of a question and more of a statement.

Angie's eyes widened. "Yes, it is. Ever since it happened, she's been acting weird, and I don't know why, but I feel like something bad is happening. I don't know, I thought maybe you could help me figure it out."

The woman just stared at her. Angie suddenly felt foolish for coming back. She assumed the woman would tell her to go home and get off the hallucinogens.

"The cat that bit her. It was ailuranthropic."

Angie was slightly taken aback by her even-keeled tone. "I don't have a clue what that means."

"It's a werecat. And now that it's bit your girlfriend, she's turning—"

"You mean a werewolf?" Angie interrupted.

"No, a were*cat*."

"What the fuck is a werecat?"

"Just what it sounds like."

"That can't possibly exist."

"But you had no trouble believing in werewolves," retorted Solange.

Angie blinked a few times. "Fair point. Please continue."

Solange sighed deeply and turned to go behind the counter. She bustled around, collecting items on the glass top, and continued speaking: "Many ancient cultures believed that people who could shift—that is, turn into animals—were actually gods in disguise. Many others thought they were witches. Whatever they were, they still linger here and there in our world—"

Suddenly, Angie interrupted the older woman. "Okay, no, that is not possible. I don't know if you're joking with me or really believe this stuff, but either way, I'm leaving. Sorry to have bothered you." She walked out of the store before Solange had time to reply.

IV

Still shaking her head, Angie marched into the Starbucks a few streets away. She ordered her tall caramel macchiato with almond milk and settled down in the corner to get some meal-planning done for her next event. The old lady at the Wiccan store was clearly crazy, but for some reason, Angie couldn't get the word "werecat" out of her head. She felt silly even considering it, but went ahead anyway, looking up search phrases such as "cat mythology" and "cat history."

She learned about a festival in Belgium called Kattenstoet that had thankfully evolved from a medieval hysteria of throwing cats out of fear that they were connected to the devil to a parade with fun, cat-themed activities. She also came across a band named Vox in Rama, after the centuries-old papal decree declaring black cats a manifestation of the devil. None of this was getting her anywhere, so with a sigh of resignation, Angie typed "werecat" into her search bar.

After scrolling through some photos of hopefully consensual furry activities, she managed to find what looked like a drawing from some centuries-old book. The caption said it was an engraving from 1793. The figure reminded her of the children's book *Where the Wild Things Are*. It was a fur-covered cat body with the face and fingers of a human.

Good ole Wikipedia informed her of the werecat's connection to witch trials in medieval Europe. Shape-shifters had been considered witches, even if they hadn't had any other magical powers. Did that mean that Missy was turning into a witch? Maybe she had been a witch all along and was only now getting her powers. Did that mean that the cat biting her had triggered those powers, or did that incident actually have nothing to do with what was happening?

Angie mentally chided herself for falling into the supernatural trap and continued scrolling through the page. According to the site, in some African folklore, shapeshifters were demigods born when gods and humans mated. Angie had met Missy's parents multiple times, and they had both seemed completely normal. She couldn't imagine a god or goddess willingly driving a station wagon.

She continued reading through to the subheading of Asia. Werecats in Asian mythology were a bit freakier, called demonic or vampiric. *Please don't let Missy be possessed by a blood-sucking demon.* Angie shook her head, admonishing herself for those decidedly unscientific thoughts. She slammed her MacBook closed and rubbed her eyes. The internet was not helping her figure out what was actually going on. Succumbing to despair, she left the coffee shop and headed back the way she'd come.

Walking with heavy but determined steps, Angie burst through the door of the Wiccan store and immediately began speaking.

"Okay, so let's pretend this isn't insane for a minute, and a random cat in an upscale boutique bit Missy, and now she's a shapeshifter of some sort. What the hell do I do with this information?"

Solange looked up. "Not a shapeshifter. You have to be born that way. When she turns, it will be permanent."

"Turns? Turns into what?" Angie's voice got higher as panic began to set in.

"That I can't say for sure. But from what I know, it's going to be something inhuman."

"Missy is going to become a monster. Is that what you're saying?" Angie asked, slamming her hands on the countertop.

"Not unless we reverse the infection first," Solange said calmly. She turned toward a pile of mismatched items that she'd collected on the countertop, inspecting each item in turn. She held up a smooth stone colored like a watermelon candy in alternating patches of green and pink. "This is unkakite jasper, one of the best crystals for healing the mind and the heart. It's good for balancing emotions and should help to calm the rapid changes."

Solange shaved some of the stone into a mortar. She went on to add some herbs spend pastes from small jars, mashing the concoction together with a pestle before dumping the suspension mixture into a strainer and pouring hot water over it. The steeped liquid was then transferred to a vial, capped, and passed over the counter to Angie.

"You need to get her to drink this. It has to be the perfect timing, though. Luckily, All Hallows Eve is only a few days away. Give it to her on Halloween night."

"How do I make her drink it?"

"That's for you to figure out. And if you don't . . ."

"If I don't, then what?

"Then you'll need this." Solange handed Angie a shiny silver instrument. Angie held it up and realized it was a small knife with a simple handle and a sharp blade. Angie stared at the woman, wide-eyed.

"If you don't stop the transformation in time, you'll have to kill the beast before she kills you. Or someone else."

"Beast?" Angie said weakly. Images of giant panthers ran through her mind, glowing eyes in the dark, just above sharp canines. "I can't kill my girlfriend," she said softly, not taking her eyes off the weapon.

"If she turns, she won't be your girlfriend anymore," Solange answered solemnly. Before Angie could retort, the shopkeeper grabbed another stone, this one rougher and striped in brown and tan. "Tiger's eye. This one's for you; it will help replace your anxiety and fear so you can remain calm."

Great, Angie thought to herself, hoping her daily dose of Prozac would be enough to counteract any bad vibes that these stones couldn't fix. She wasn't the praying type, but if she had been, she would have been praying that she could stop Missy from turning into this thing before she even had to consider using the blade in her bag.

V

Halloween night was rainy and drab, with signs of a thunderstorm on the horizon. Carefully constructed displays of witch's cauldrons and vampire caskets were falling apart under the soggy mist of the air, and the once brightly colored leaves in the gutters had turned to a dull brown. The rain started to trickle down as three almost-too-old trick-or-treaters yelled thanks and left their porch.

"Two more zombies and a hippie!" Angie shouted back at Missy as she closed the door on the latest group. It was always their tradition to keep track of all the costumes they saw at their front door, but this year, Missy didn't even glance at most of the kids who graced their doorstep.

The timer on the oven beeped. Angie set the plastic jack-o-lantern half full of candy down on the stairs and moved into the living room, where one of the *Halloween* sequels was playing on TV. Missy wasn't really paying attention but rather staring off into space.

"Dinner?" she asked.

Missy nodded almost robotically, then got up, followed her girlfriend into the kitchen, and sat down. Angie took the casserole out of the oven and served them both. She had made her not-quite-famous vegan pumpkin lasagna, a dish that her better half normally couldn't get enough of. Tonight, however, Missy seemed to just push the food around her plate.

Suddenly, Missy started coughing violently, frantically grabbing at her glass of water until the spasms subsided.

"Oh my god, a hairball," Angie gasped softly, not realizing she'd spoken aloud.

"What?" Missy looked across at her, annoyed.

"Nothing," Angie quickly responded, moving just a few centimeters back in her chair. Angie focused intently on her dinner plate, trying to calm her rapid pulse. Missy was scratching at her arm again despite the fact that the wound was nearly healed already. Angie had given up trying to get her to stop, as each urging was met with more and more hostility.

Angie got up from the table and set out a cerulean coffee mug. She pulled the vial out from its hiding place in her bra, tipped it into the mug, and quickly shoved the empty glass back into her shirt. She added an herbal tea bag and poured hot water into the mug from the kettle that had been slowly simmering.

"You should drink this," Angie said in what she hoped was a totally normal voice, placing the mug down in front of her girlfriend. "I got it from Whole Foods; it's supposed to be good for healing."

Missy just stared at her, barely moving.

Angie cleared her throat. "I figured it could help with the cat bite? Plus, it tastes good."

Still no response.

"Babe, please, humor me?"

After a beat, Missy picked up the mug and sipped from it.

A crack of thunder broke through the room, followed by a flickering of the lights before they turned off completely.

A flash of lightning illuminated the kitchen, and Angie noticed with a cold feeling of dread that her girlfriend was no longer sitting across from her. For a second, she thought she saw Missy's eyes shining across the room, but then everything went back to blackness.

Without the background noise of the television or refrigerator, the quiet was only broken by the pattering of rain and smaller peals of thunder.

"M-M-M-Missy?" Angie stammered.

She screamed as a dark shape jumped nearby, but then she realized it wasn't headed for her. Instead, her girlfriend was crouched on the floor, retching. She took one last heave as the contents of her stomach—including Solange's concoction—left her body for the linoleum floor.

Shit, Angie thought.

Missy tried to stand, staggering as her body fought for balance.

"Babe?" Angie tentatively reached out an arm to help her, but Missy began convulsing on the other side of the kitchen.

Another flash of lighting showed Angie a huddled shape that didn't resemble a human or a cat. In the dark, she could see the body bending and stretching. With horror, she took tentative steps forward.

"Missy. I'm here, it's okay," she said softly, approaching the writhing mass.

A sound cut through the air that made Angie scream and jump back to crouch behind the kitchen island. It was not unlike the screech of a stray cat, but with more pain and, somehow, more humanity.

Everything was dark again. The lightning seemed to have subsided, but Angie wished it would come back so she could see what was going on. Taking a deep breath, she worked the blade out of her pocket and began to crawl toward her girlfriend once more.

"Missy?" She crept around the corner of the island that was blocking her view, shakily holding out the silver knife in front of her. As her eyes slowly adjusted to the dark, she came to a horrible realization. Where her five-foot-eight girlfriend had before been crouched and trembling on the floor, there was instead something else.

It was a cat. Not a monstrous being from an old horror movie with sharp fangs. Just a normal, everyday housecat. Angie locked eyes with the ten-pound feline, immediately recognizing the hazel hue. She lowered the weapon in shock.

"Missy?" she asked quietly, flicking the lights back on.

The cat—a brown tabby, she could now tell—meowed sweetly and walked toward her. Angie froze as the animal began rubbing up against her. She let out a breath she hadn't realized she'd been holding and dropped the knife to the floor.

Angie pulled the fuzzy creature onto her lap and scratched its head.

"It's okay, baby. I've got you."

About the Author

Jamie Zaccaria works full-time as a science writer doing communications for an ocean exploration organization. She writes fiction and nonfiction in her spare time and also enjoys lobbying for important causes, making weird art projects, and hanging out with her pitbull and cats. She lives in New Jersey with her wife.

Publication History

- "The Witch of the Woods" was originally published in *Night Terrors Vol. 3* by Scare Street (September 2020).

- "A Necessary Procedure" was originally published in *The Bitchin' Kitsch* (April 2021).

- "Comatose Beauty" was originally published in *The Gray Sisters* (June 2020).

- "A Killer Brunch Special" was originally published in *Gluttony* by Black Hare Press (March 2021).

- "Eviscerate" was originally published in Danse Macabre's *DM du Jour* (December 2020).

- "Lips as Red as Blood" was originally published in *Demonic Classics: Once Upon A Debacle* by Battle Goddess Productions (September 2020).

- "Personal Demons" was originally published in *The Siren's Call* (Halloween 2020) and again in *Ankh Quarterly* (Fall 2020).

- "The Crukker" was originally published in *Hookman and Friends* by DBND Publishing (August 2020).

* "Orca" was originally published in *Literary Veganism* (August 2020) and republished as the third-place winner of *Tiny Seed Literary Journal's* Through the Eyes of Nature Contest (October 2020).

* "The Devil Down in Jersey" was originally published in *From The Yonder Volume* 2 by War Monkey Publications (March 2021).

* "Salt" was originally published in *Whigmaleeries & Wives' Tales* by JayHenge Publishing (September 2020).

* "Conversations in the Back of an Uber" was originally published in *Tipping the Scales Literary Journal* (Christmas 2020).

* "Cat Scratch Fever" was originally published in *Triangle Writers Magazine* (May 2020).